"What is this urgent task you require of me?"

"It's a simple matter." Her fists balled inside her long sleeves. "Once it's done, you may leave Fortemur a free man, well horsed and supplied with sword, lance and shield from the castle armory."

He did not leap at the offer. Jocelyn would not have trusted him if he had. This one, she'd sensed from the moment he'd stood tall and defiant on the auction block, would break before he'd bend.

"What do you want of me?"

Very well. He wished it without bard or barding. So be it.

"I want you to lie with me."

He reared back. "What say you?"

"I want you in my bed this night, and this night only. Then you will leave Fortemur with all I promised you."

Suspicion warred with incredulity in his face. "Why?"

"The reason is not your concern," she said haughtily.

He looked her up and down with an insolence that brought the blood rushing to her cheeks.

* * *

Crusader Captive

Harlequin® Historical #1050—July 2011

Author Note

Okay, I admit it. I've always been fascinated by tales of knights and ladies fair. So fascinated that I wrote several novels set during the reigns of Eleanor of Aquitaine and her son, Richard the Lionhearted.

But none of the research I did into their times and the great Crusades that shaped their lives came anywhere close to the incredible experience of visiting the same places Eleanor and Richard had journeyed to. The moment I stepped off the tour bus and viewed Jerusalem from the Mount of Olives, I was lost in the awe-inspiring history of the city. And when I walked up the ramparts of Saladin's great citadel in Cairo, I knew I had to set another book during the era of the Crusades.

So here it is, the tale of a knight pledged to the Templars and the lady who forces him to choose between duty and desire, with the fate of an entire kingdom hanging in the balance. I thoroughly enjoyed watching their story play out against such a rich historical tapestry. Hope you do, too!

Crusader Captive

MERLINE LOVELACE

TORONTO NEW YORK LONDON
AMSTERDAM PARIS SYDNEY HAMBURG
STOCKHOLM ATHENS TOKYO MILAN MADRID
PRAGUE WARSAW BUDAPEST AUCKLAND

Recycling programs
for this product may
not exist in your area.

ISBN-13: 978-0-373-29650-7

CRUSADER CAPTIVE

This edition published by arrangement with Harlequin Books S.A.

For questions and comments about the quality of this book please contact us at Customer_eCare@Harlequin.ca.

www.Harlequin.com

Printed in U.S.A.

Available from Harlequin® Historical and
MERLINE LOVELACE

Silhouette Romantic Suspense

**Diamonds Can Be Deadly* #1411
**Closer Encounters* #1439
**Stranded with a Spy* #1483
**Match Play* #1500
**Undercover Wife* #1531
**Seduced by the Operative* #1589
**Risky Engagement* #1613
**Danger in the Desert* #1640
**Strangers When We Meet* #1660

Coming soon
**Double Deception* #1667

Nocturne

Mind Games #37
†*Time Raiders: The Protector* #75

Silhouette Desire

**Devlin and the Deep Blue Sea* #1726
***The CEO's Christmas Proposition* #1905
***The Duke's New Year's Resolution* #1913
***The Executive's Valentine's Seduction* #1917

*Code Name: Danger
**Holidays Abroad
†Time Raiders

To my own sexy knight in shining armor.
Thanks for all the fabulous adventures, my darling.

Chapter One

The port city of El-Arish, on the much-disputed border between the Caliphate of Cairo and the Latin Kingdom of Jerusalem, Anno Domini 1152

"That one."

Her entire face hidden behind a veil after the style of women of the East, Lady Jocelyn tipped a nod toward the wretch who'd been hauled from the slave pens. It took two burly guards armed with pikes to prod the man onto the auction block. Despite his shackles, he was of a size to be reckoned with.

"My lady!"

Her castellan's protest was low and for her ears only. Sir Hugh had journeyed to Outremer years ago with Jocelyn's grandfather. He was somewhat grizzled of late but had lost little of his strength and none of his ability to wield a sword. Like Jocelyn, he'd donned Eastern garb for this dangerous excursion across the ever-fluctuating border between the two kingdoms. His hooded robe shielded most of his face as he leaned closer to the lady he'd sworn to serve.

"But look at the bruises on that one's arms and face. They bespeak a stubborn, intractable nature. He'll never bend to your will."

"He has no choice. Not if he wishes his freedom."

That was true enough. Ever since the Pope had declared a second Crusade seven years ago, thousands upon thousands of would-be warriors for Christ had swelled the ranks of pilgrims making the perilous journey to the Holy Land. Even Louis VII of France and his wife, Eleanor of Aquitaine, had answered the call. Although they'd returned to France after a somewhat less than successful campaign, their daring exploits—and scandalous affairs—had become the stuff of legend in Outremer.

Unfortunately, the ranks of those who preyed on travelers making the hazardous trek had swelled as well. So many pilgrims and Crusaders had fallen victim to brigands and pirates that the slave markets from Cairo to Damascus were flooded with pale-skinned Franks. Even here, on the very border of the Latin kingdom that had been their destination when they had set out months or years ago, so many came on the auction block that prices had dropped like lead weights.

Jocelyn wished fervently she could buy them all. She and her grandfather before her had sent agents to purchase many of these hapless captives until tensions escalated and the Fatamids of Egypt had closed their borders. It was a measure of her desperation that she'd made this risky foray to purchase a slave she could use to achieve her ends.

If she could use him. Her castellan seemed most doubtful.

"But look at him," Sir Hugh urged. "For all his bruises, he is roped with muscle and sinew."

He was indeed! Through the slit in her veil, Jocelyn inspected the slave on the auction block. Beneath his matted hair and filthy beard no doubt crawling with lice, he displayed a body that told her this was no mere pilgrim. No lowly plowman or tradesman eager to win everlasting salvation by answering the Pope's call. Such muscled shoulders, such a flat belly and taut, corded thighs bespoke years of hard training and rigorous discipline. He'd swung a sword, she guessed shrewdly, and swung it often.

But it was his stance that intrigued her. Shoulders square, chin angled, he stood with his feet spread as far as his leg irons would allow and looked out on the noisy crowd with disdain in his astonishingly blue eyes. If she must use a slave to achieve her purposes, she decided, she would as lief not use a sniveling, cowardly one.

Then his gaze caught hers, or seemed to. Scorn rippled across his face and curled his lip. Jocelyn bristled at the sneer even as she acknowledged the reason behind it. Veiled and robed in a voluminous cloak as she was, he took her for a woman of the East. Come, like the other females in the noisy crowd, to inspect and taunt the latest Frankish captives put on the block.

Ever after Jocelyn would wonder whether it was the contempt on his face that sealed his fate—and hers. Or whether her decision was driven by the contrariness that had so delighted her grandfather and caused a long succession of nurses to shake their heads in dismay. Whatever the reason, she'd made her choice. This one would serve her purposes, she vowed silently, say he or nay he.

And despite his rags and matted hair, she had to admit this tall, unbending captive was more pleasing to the eye than most males. Certainly more pleasing than the first man she'd been promised to in marriage. Dark and most dour of visage, Lord Reynaud could have counted forty winters to her five at the time of their betrothal. But he'd brought Jocelyn sweets and baubles, and she had accepted without question that she would wed a man closer to her grandfather's age than hers.

It was her duty, after all. From the time she was

old enough to grasp such matters, Jocelyn had understood that she must contract an alliance with a knight strong enough to hold the lands and massive, fortified castle overlooking the Mediterranean Sea that were her birthright. Lord Reynaud had been just such a fearsome warrior.

When he had taken an arrow through the eye at the siege of Antioch, Jocelyn's grandfather had sought another mate for her. A much younger lord this time, but no less valiant. Laughing, merry-eyed Geoffrey de Lusignan had been the embodiment of all Jocelyn's girlish dreams. She had made her vows eagerly, but she had been deemed still too young to consummate the marriage. Her heart had near broke when Geoffrey, too, went down in battle.

She'd matured rapidly in mind and body after that. So much so that her grandsire had agreed it was time she went to a husband's bed. He'd been negotiating yet another strategic alliance when he had succumbed to a bloody flux of the bowels and his grieving granddaughter had became ward to Baldwin the Third, King of Jerusalem.

And what a turbulent wardship it had been! Twelve months and more of political wrangling, with Jocelyn caught squarely in the middle.

Only a little older than Jocelyn herself, Baldwin had spent most of those twelve months defending his kingdom against the enemies who besieged it on all sides. At the same time, he'd been forced to struggle mightily to wrest power from his mother. Queen Melisande had ruled the Kingdom of Jerusalem for more than two decades and was loath to relinquish the reins now that her son had come of age. So intense had their struggle become that Baldwin had been forced to besiege his lady mother and her loyal followers in Jerusalem before they'd worked out a tentative peace.

As one of the wealthiest heiresses in the kingdom, Jocelyn had become a pawn—nay, a hapless mouse—batted between the paws of those two royal lions. So many matches had been proposed for her before being struck down by either the king or his strong-willed mother that she'd lost count.

But this last…

By all that was holy, this last! And to think both Melisande and her son favored the match!

Beneath her enveloping cloak, a shudder rippled down Jocelyn's spine. She understood the twisted politics that pitted kin against kin and Christian against other Christians in a kingdom struggling mightily for its very survival. She should, having been born and bred in the turbulent East. What's more, she fully acknowledged the need for strategic alliances wherever possible with powerful Saracen lords.

But she would be damned if she would go meekly into the bed of the Emir of Damascus. Ali ben Haydar was known throughout the East for his predilection for tender young virgins. Once he'd pierced their maiden's shield, he consigned them to his harem and rarely, if ever, called them to his bed again. At last count, more than three hundred of his wives and concubines languished in luxurious boredom.

Not Jocelyn! Baldwin and his mother could find another untried maid to send to the emir's bed. She would use this unkempt slave as the instrument of her delivery from the harem.

"That one," she instructed Sir Hugh. "Go quickly. Offer gold to the auctioneer before he opens the bidding to all. I want to be back across the border before dark."

"Milady..."

"Go!"

Jocelyn had acted as chatelaine for her grandfather almost from the day she'd put off short skirts and could totter around the castle at his heels. Her vassals and servants knew her every gesture, her every tone. This one brooked no further argument, even from the knight who'd served as castellan to both her and her grandsire.

"Aye, milady."

Sir Hugh signaled to the equerries who'd accompanied them across the border. He'd chosen each man carefully. Of Eastern descent, they wore their native robes to disguise the fact they'd sworn allegiance to a Frankish lord. Jocelyn's grandfather had enlisted many such men in his service, and they now served her with fierce, unswerving devotion. Such were the convoluted, complex and ever-changing loyalties of Outremer.

"Sulim, you and Omar will come with me," Hugh ordered. "Hanrah, escort our lady back to the horses and wait for me there."

Jocelyn threw a last look at her prospective purchase. The slanting afternoon sun cast his body in bronze. His tall, square-shouldered and most defiant body.

A spear of doubt lanced through her. And something else. Something that tightened her chest and stirred an unfamiliar heat low in her belly.

Untried maid though she was, she recognized the odd sensation. No girl could grow to womanhood in a crowded keep without understanding what drove dairymaids to lift their skirts to stable hands and knights to rut with willing kitchen wenches. It was lust, pure and simple, of a sort that would earn Jocelyn a heavy penance from the castle priest when she confessed it.

If she confessed it. Her plan was so dangerous, her intentions so outrageous, that she'd confided them to no one but Sir Hugh. Her conscience wouldn't allow her to put any other of her people at risk, not even the kindly, if somewhat absentminded, priest who served as her confessor.

Suddenly, the enormity of what she contemplated almost overwhelmed her. Dear sweet savior! Was she mad to even think that she might change the course of her future? That she could defy a king? Torn, she came within a breath of abandoning the scheme Sir Hugh kept insisting was foolhardy and hazardous in the extreme.

But her castellan had already left her side and was threading his way through the crowd to the auctioneer's table. Jocelyn bit her lip, wavered a moment more, then turned on her heel.

Simon de Rhys ignored the raw agony of his wounds and stood rigid with shame. Flies swarmed around his head and bit at the oozing lash marks on his back. Wrist and ankle cuffs cut into his flesh. He said not a word as a sun-weathered man draped from head to foot in a hooded cloak dropped coins into the palm of the slave merchant. Yet of all the indignities he'd suffered in the past year, this was the worst.

He'd answered the call, albeit reluctantly, when summoned to the sickbed of the father whose scheming ways had lost the family both lands and honor.

He'd listened in cynical disbelief when Gervase de Rhys had rasped that he regretted his many sins and had pledged his youngest son to the Knights Templar as penance.

He'd done his damnedest to ignore that pledge until the saintly Bishop of Clairvaux had pointed out that Simon would imperil his own soul if he didn't fulfill his father's vow.

And he'd fought like a wild beast when pirates had

overrun the ship transporting him and a boatload of other travelers to the Holy Land, then endured the vicious bite of a lead-tipped lash as his captors tried to whip him into submission.

But this…

This scraped away what little was left of his pride. Jaw tight, he tried not to think of the rich prizes his strong arm had won in tournaments. Nor of the ransoms he'd collected from the knights he'd bested in battle. He was no longer Simon de Rhys, champion in more lists than he could count. He'd turned all his earthly possessions over to the Church, as required of members of the Order of the Poor Knights of Christ and the Temple of Solomon. And this despite the fact he was as yet only an aspirant to the order. There hadn't been time for him to undergo the Templars' secret initiation rituals before he took ship to the Holy Land. Now he was a slave to the very infidels he'd sworn to defeat! The bitter, inescapable fact ate at him like sharp-beaked ravens pecking at his entrails.

Stiff of spine, he ignored the heckling noises from the crowd as coins changed hands, ignored the pain of his lacerated back, ignored all until his new master beckoned imperiously for him to follow. Chains clanking, he hobbled back to the pens crammed with despairing captives.

Once there, the slave master struck off his leg irons. He refused to wince as the man knocked the pins from the cuffs with callous indifference, but fiery pain seared his bruised and bloodied ankles. Teeth gritted, Simon locked his hands together and contemplated a last, desperate act. He was too weak from lack of sustenance to acquit himself in a full-pitched battle, but he could still swing his wrist chain in a deadly arc.

He would not get far. Not in this crowded market-place. Simon accepted that. But he would die fighting, as he'd sworn to do when he'd accepted the burden of his sire's pledge. He had intertwined his fingers and was poised for attack when his new master issued a terse command.

"Follow me."

Simon blinked. Had he heard aright? Had the man addressed him in his own tongue? In a pure accent that marked him unmistakably as a Frank?

"Who are you?"

"You will learn in good time," the man growled. "Come, we must make haste."

Simon's thoughts chased around and around, like a dog after its own tail. He could still swing the length of wrist chain. Still crush a skull or two or three before he was taken down. Or he could follow this man and see where he led...

He led to a small but well-armed cavalcade waiting in the shadow of the city's walls. Simon's pulse leaped at his first glimpse of a midnight-black Arabian steed that looked as though he would run with the wind. It leaped again when he saw who straddled the courser's back.

The woman from the marketplace. Despite her hooded cloak and the veil that obscured everything but her eyes, he'd recognized her immediately. She'd stood taller than the others of her sex, and straighter. As if used to holding her head up among men instead of bending it in proper subservience.

He'd seen how she'd appraised him, like a fishwife looking over the day's catch. Was she wife to the man who'd bought him? Daughter? Would she expect Simon to bow and scrape? Not while he had a breath left in him, he vowed with a touch of the same scorn that had curled his lip when he'd caught her gaze in the marketplace.

The woman's eyes narrowed but she said not a word as his new master gestured to a dun-colored barb shifting restlessly at the end of its reins.

"Mount," the man ordered tersely, "and get you a good seat in the saddle. We've a hard ride ahead."

"Where do we ride?"

"That's not your concern. Mount."

Despite his manacled wrists, Simon swung into the saddle with the ease of one more used to being ahorse than afoot. It galled him no little that he wasn't allowed to take the reins. Those were held fast by a heathen in a white turban.

He'd barely found the stirrups before his new master set off. The female rode at his side. Simon and the guard holding his reins followed, with two more turbaned outriders bringing up the rear.

They halted at the city gates, where the one who'd bought him slipped a handful of coins to the pikemen guarding the entrance. Once clear of the mud huts surrounding the city they gained a well-traveled highway. Steep hills blanketed with olive trees bordered the road on the left. The sea stretched endlessly on the right.

The sun hanging low over the azure waters told Simon they were headed north. But north to where? Frowning, he struggled to draw on his hazy grasp of the geography of the East.

The Latin Kingdom of Jerusalem was little more than a narrow strip of land squeezed between desert, mountain and sea. A much-beleaguered strip, to be sure, wrested from its original inhabitants during the First Crusade a mere fifty years ago. From the bits and pieces he'd been able to gather from his captors, Simon knew that the city they'd just left lay somewhere close to the kingdom's border. If this troop continued to ride north, they would come even closer.

Close enough that he might find sanctuary if he escaped. When he escaped, he amended fiercely. He hadn't come all this way to spend the rest of his life in chains. He might be the fifth son of a minor and most disreputable baron, but he'd won more battles than he'd lost. This one, he vowed grimly, was not yet over.

His hope of escape rose with each thud of his mount's hooves, only to be dashed some moments later like the waves crashing against the rocks below. News traveled so slowly between East and West. The infidels could well have taken the southern reaches of the Latin Kingdom, just as they'd taken the great principality of Edessa to the north, the loss of which had precipitated the Second Crusade. For all Simon knew, even that most sacred of all Christian sites, the Church of the Holy Sepulchre in Jerusalem, could have fallen.

The mere thought made his insides churn. He'd come so far. To fulfill his father's vow and salvage his own soul, he must find some means to complete the last leg of his journey and join the ranks of Templars. He was sorting through various strategies when his new master stiffened in the saddle.

"Fatamids," he grunted in a voice just loud enough to carry over the restless murmur of the sea.

Simon narrowed his eyes against the sun's glare and studied the mounted patrol some distance ahead. Their conical helmets identified them as readily as the Arabic symbols on their blood-red pennant. He expected his new master to approach them, mayhap hand over more coins as tariff for using the road. To his amazement, the woman took charge.

"They fly the pennant of the sultan's personal

regiment," he heard her mutter. "If they stop us, we won't be able to bribe them as we did the guards at the city gates."

"Especially if they recognize you, milady," the man beside her agreed grimly.

So this veiled female was a Frank, and one of high rank. Simon barely had time to absorb those astounding facts before she cast a look over her shoulder. He caught a glimpse of brown eyes blazing with determination as she measured the mettle of her escort.

"I know these hills and orchards well," she told them in an urgent tone. "Guy of Bures held them in fief before he lost them to the Fatamids. I spent nigh on one summer here with Guy's wife and daughters. Follow where I lead."

Before any could protest, she tugged on the reins and dug her heels into her mount's sides. The sleek Arabian leaped off the road. Its rider canted well forward in her saddle and sent it racing toward the olive trees that climbed the steep hillside.

Cursing, the man Simon now recognized as the woman's lieutenant dragged his mount's head around and charged after her. Simon was forced to cling to the saddle like a hapless monkey as he and the rest of the troop followed. Gnarled, twisted tree trunks blackened by age flashed by. Ancient boughs feathered with silver leaves whipped past. He ducked two branches, was lashed by a third.

Over the hammer of iron-shod hooves on the

rocky soil, he heard a distant shout. A glance over his shoulder confirmed that the sultan's troop was giving chase. His trained eye saw at once it was well armed and well horsed.

The fire of battle rose in him. His manacled hands curled tight, as if to grip a lance or sword. He told himself he should care not whose hands he passed into. A slave was a slave was a slave. Yet everything in him rebelled at the idea of being caught weaponless if there was to be a battle. Cursing, he swung forward in his saddle—and felt his heart near jump out of his throat.

They'd reached the crest of the hill. In an instant of sheer disbelief, Simon saw it was slashed by what looked like a bottomless crevasse. The gaping fissure stretched in either direction as far as he could see. And the only means to cross it was a wood-and-hemp bridge that looked as though it would not support a shoat, let alone a horse and rider.

The female in the lead dragged on the reins and brought her mount to a snorting, skittering stop. When she threw her leg over the pommel and slid from the saddle, Simon was sure she meant to surrender. Instead, she issued a hurried assurance.

"The bridge will take us. I crossed it more than once with Sir Guy and his wife. Wait until I gain the other side, then follow one at a time."

"No, lady!" Her sun-weathered lieutenant kicked

free of the stirrups. Dismounting, he shouldered her aside. "I will go first."

Simon's breath stuck to the back of his throat as the man led his mount onto the swaying bridge. The damned thing looked as though it would give way at any second, taking man and beast with it.

Against all odds, they made it to the far side. And no sooner had they reached solid ground than the woman followed. She crossed safely, as did one of the turbaned outriders.

That left Simon and two others. The first dragged him out of his saddle. The second flung his mount's reins at him and drew a curved scimitar.

"Go," he ordered, his voice low and guttural with menace.

Simon had no fear of heights. He'd climbed many a siege tower and fought atop high castle walls. Yet he held back, debating between evils.

He could swing his wrist chain, knock the scimitar aside, and take to the trees in hopes of escaping both this troop and the one charging up the hill.

Or he could put his fate in the hands of the female who stood on the other side, her gaze once again locked with his.

Those fierce brown eyes challenged him. Bedeviled him. Lured him to God knew what fate. With the grim sensation that he was putting more than his life in this most strange and unaccountable female's hands, Simon led the dun-colored barb onto the bridge.

It sagged under their weight, but held. Simon forced himself to place one foot before the other and kept his eyes on the lady. Neither he nor she seemed to draw breath until he gained the far side.

As soon as he had, the remaining two followed. All the while, the pursuing troop drew closer. They were almost within arrow range when the grizzled lieutenant drew his sword. Two whacks severed the right-side ropes anchoring the bridge to deep-sunk posts. The planks tipped on their side, swinging like a drunken sailor caught in the rigging.

"They won't cross now," the lieutenant said with fierce satisfaction.

"No, they won't," his lady agreed gleefully.

With lithe grace and a swirl of her voluminous cloak, she grasped her saddle pommel and swung into the seat unaided.

"To horse," she ordered over the thunder of approaching hooves. "Let us home to Fortemur."

Chapter Two

By the time the small cavalcade thundered up to the barbican of a massive castle overlooking the sea, the sun was a flaming ball of red and Simon had to struggle to hold his head upright.

As best he could recall, all he'd eaten since being dragged off the ship two days ago were a few wormy crusts of bread. Worse than the hunger that gnawed at his insides, though, was the burning cauldron of his back. His captors' lead-tipped whips had cut almost to the bone.

Yet training and instinct refused to die. With an iron effort of will, he blanked his mind to the pain that ate near into his bones and fixed his gaze on the black-and-red pennants flying above the keep's towers. He didn't recognize the device on them, nor the coat of arms carved into stone above the gate of the outer barbican.

When they passed through the gates and crossed the drawbridge, he acknowledged grimly that the fortress well deserved its name. Fortemur. Strong walls. It had those aplenty. And guardsmen, as well. He glimpsed pairs of lookouts in the dozen or more towers interspaced along the walls, while more pikemen in red-and-black tabards patrolled the walks between.

The towers were of a unique design that owed as much to the East as to the West. Almost like the minarets that called the infidels to worship. They gave the massive keep an almost fanciful air that belied its well-ordered defenses.

Its outer and inner curtain walls were spaced well apart, he noted. Gardens and orchards flowered in the low-lying land between them. They would feed the defenders during a lengthy siege. Until the outer curtain was breached, at least. Then, Simon surmised, the defenders would open the sea gates and flood the orchards to keep attackers at bay.

He gave the yards the same reluctant approval. Both inner and outer bailey teamed with activity from the dovecote to the farrier's forge to the kitchens that pumped the tantalizing odor of roasted meat into the air. Simon's stomach cried for a slice of whatever sizzled on the spits as the troop halted by the stables and the lady slid from her saddle.

She spared him only a glance before throwing back her hood and issuing a low order to her lieutenant. "See him fed and bathed, then bring him to my solar."

Simon barely heard her. Although the silken veil still covered most of her face, he couldn't help but gape at the thick braid draped over one shoulder. It was so pale a gold as to be almost luminous. Like winter sunlight shimmering on a frozen lake. Simon had never seen the like.

With some effort, he dragged his gaze from her to her lieutenant. He'd shoved back his hood as well. The man's weathered face owed more to age than the sun, Simon now saw. Silver tinted his hair at the temples. And the scar running from his ear to the neck of his tunic bespoke a man who'd engaged in more than one battle. Some, obviously, with the female he now faced.

"Do you want him with the wrist cuffs on or off?" he queried in a voice tinged with unmistakable disapproval.

She directed her attention to Simon and raked him again from head to foot. As he had on the auction block, he stiffened under her assessing look.

By the bones of Saint Bartholomew, she was a forward wench. The kind whose bold glance would have raised an answering response from him in other times, other circumstances. He'd bedded his share and more of saucy maids and painted, panting ladies before his father's dying vow had bound him to a life of poverty, obedience and chastity.

Yet he'd never encountered a female such as this one. Strong enough to ride for hours without so much as slumping in the saddle. Strong-willed enough to issue orders to the battle-scarred veteran who awaited her command.

"Off," she told him. "But you have my leave to subdue him if he offers violence."

"He'd best not."

Simon knew the gruff response was more for his benefit than hers. She knew it, as well. She turned away with a nod, then swung back.

"Be sure to bring him to me by way of the tower stairs."

"I will."

Simon's gaze followed her as she lifted her skirts and stepped around the offal inevitable in a stable yard teeming with horses, swine and chickens. She had a fine-turned ankle, he couldn't help but note before he faced her lieutenant once again.

"I am Hugh of Poitiers," the man informed him. "Once in service to Eleanor of Aquitaine. For these past two decades and more, I am sworn to the holder of these lands."

"Who is he?"

"She." Sir Hugh tipped his head to the retreating female. "Lady Jocelyn is my liege."

Simon's glance whipped to the lady, then back again. "She holds this keep? She has no husband? No father or brother?"

"She has me," the knight snapped.

"I meant no offense. But a fortress of this size..."

When his glance swept the well-ordered yards again, Sir Hugh offered a terse explanation.

"Lady Jocelyn's grandfather died this Michaelmas past, before he could negotiate a suitable marriage for her. King Baldwin took her in as his ward and appointed one of his own men as steward. The fool likes to believe he holds sway here. I would suggest you do not make the same mistake."

So that was the way of it. The lady was an heiress. A prize to be given to a faithful vassal. From the looks of this keep, she was a rich prize indeed.

Simon knew well—all Christendom did—that the constant struggle to hold on to the territories wrested from the Saracens in the First Crusade had caused many a lord to fall on the field of battle. Their sons likewise often went down to the sword or lance. As a result, great fiefs devolved on female heirs here in the East far more often than in the West. Tales abounded of rich widows being given to new husbands almost before they'd buried their last.

Such rumors had lured many a landless knight and adventurous man-at-arms to seek both a bride and a fortune here in Outremer. Simon himself had considered doing so, but he would not now make a fortune nor take a bride in this wild land. Both were forbidden to Knights Templar. All they took in spoils, all revenues they gained through their vast holdings both here and in the West, belonged to the order.

"How are you known?" Sir Hugh wanted to know.

"I am Simon de Rhys, fifth son of Gervase de Rhys."

"Gervase de Rhys." The knight's brow wrinkled. "What have I heard of him?"

That he was foresworn of his honor, his lands and the respect of all men, Simon thought bitterly. That he whored and guzzled ale and took by guile what he could not take by the strength of his arm. It wasn't by chance that Simon had ridden away from his sire's crumbling keep soon as he'd been strong enough to swing a sword and not returned until summoned to the man's deathbed.

His shoulders stiffening, he answered only, "I know not."

"How old are you?"

"Six and twenty."

Hugh's eyes narrowed. "Have you won your spurs?"

"Ten years ago."

"So young?" Surprised, the scarred warrior raked him with a sharp look. "By whose hand were you knighted?"

"Henri, Duke of Angoulême."

"Ah, him I have heard of. He was a good man. If he knighted you, you must have won his respect."

Hugh stroked his chin for several moments, his piercing gaze seeming to see into Simon's soul.

"I heartily disapprove of what Lady Jocelyn has in store for you," he said at last, "but understand why she does it. Whether you fall in with her plans or no, hear me well, Simon de Rhys. I will rip you and string you up by your guts should you harm one hair on her head."

"I—"

He flung up a mailed fist. "I care not what you say or think! Only that you know your life is forfeit if you harm her. Do you understand me?"

"Yes."

"Then let us get you fed and bathed, as my lady commanded. Then I will take you to her solar."

Jocelyn paced the spacious tower room, her nerves strung so tight she feared they would snap.

Until her grandfather's death she'd shared a bedchamber with the other unmarried ladies of the keep. Four, sometimes six, of them had slept in the curtained bed, the rest on the cushioned benches they sat on during the day to sew or read or strum their lutes. Now that she'd moved into the lord's chamber, Jocelyn enjoyed the almost unheard-of luxury of privacy. That privacy allowed her to do what she was determined to do this night!

She'd planned her campaign with the same care Sir Hugh did an attack on enemy strongholds. With the sun about to set, she'd ordered candles and a fire laid. Stout wood shutters now shut out the night and the chill breeze coming off the sea. Rich tapestries kept drafts from seeping through the stone walls, while thick carpets covered the wooden floorboards. The chamber was warm and comfortable, yet her nerves danced and her skin shivered as though she was clothed in nothing but a thin shift.

Yet just the opposite was true! She'd thrown off her hooded cloak and sweat-stained riding gown, washed, and dressed again with great care. A simple linen band drawn across the top of her head and under her chin held back the unbound hair that now fell loose to her waist. Over a finely pleated linen undertunic she wore a bliaut of deepest rose that laced at the sides and boasted sleeves so long their tips trailed the carpets. A broad belt embroidered with gold thread girdled her hips. From it dangled her needle case, her sewing scissors in their leather holder, a pierced gold scent-ball filled with costly musk and the heavy ring of keys that marked her as chatelaine.

Once properly garbed, she'd dismissed her ladies. Sent away even the young page who customarily slept on a pallet outside her door. Jocelyn wanted none to know what passed between her and the man she would soon face.

It was mad, this scheme. As Sir Hugh had pointed out so forcefully, she courted the wrath of both King Baldwin and his still-powerful mother, Queen

Melisande. Yet she could not, would not, be shut away in a harem. She was too used to governing the lands and castle that were her birthright.

She knew the match with the Emir of Damascus was a brilliant one in terms of political alliances. By giving her to ben Haydar, Baldwin would secure the western borders of his kingdom while he battled the incursions of the Seljuk Turks to the north and the Fatamids to the south.

The emir, in turn, would gain access to the sea for the heavily laden caravans that crossed his vast holdings. In addition to land-passage fees, caravaneers would now have to pay him exorbitant port taxes as well. By taking Jocelyn to wife, the emir would double the gold and silver pouring into his coffers.

She would not be the first Frankish lady given to an Eastern lord to achieve a political or strategic advantage. The Pope himself had endorsed the marriage of Margaret of Cilicia and the Sultan of Rum to secure a buffer between Constantinople and the ever more powerful Turks. Like Lady Margaret, Jocelyn would be allowed to follow the tenets of her own faith. That the emir had solemnly promised.

And no wonder, she thought scornfully. The man took wives and concubines of every color and creed. He cared not what gods they prayed to as long as they came fresh and virginal to his bed.

Jocelyn wasn't foolish enough to think she could govern her fate completely. She knew she would have to bow her head and accept some other husband of the king's choosing. Any other husband, as long as he was of her faith and strong enough to hold Fortemur. But she would not—

The rap of knuckles on the tower door cut off her turbulent thoughts. Her breath caught. Her heart pounded. It was now, she thought with a flutter of panic, or never.

Now! It must be now.

The jewel-toned carpeting that could be purchased for a handful of beasants in every Eastern bazaar muffled her footsteps as she crossed the spacious chamber. Her hand shaking, she turned the iron key in the lock and tugged open the door to the tower stairs.

The winding stone staircase was narrow and dark, lit only by a single flickering torch set in an iron bracket and the moonbeams that came through the arrow slits. Yet there was light enough and more for her to make out Sir Hugh's disapproving expression and the tight, unreadable one on the face of the man with him.

Jocelyn stepped back to allow them entry to her chamber. The captive entered first. His matted, filthy beard had been cut off and the bristles pumiced away. His equally foul hair had been washed until it glinted a dull gold. He wore clean breeks and a coarse wool tunic, Jocelyn saw.

Standing this close to her, he loomed as tall as the

cedars from the forests of Lebanon. Her airy chamber seemed to shrink in size as he took a stance before her, his feet planted wide and his gaze intent on her face. Now that she could see his features clearly, she found him more daunting than she would admit, even to herself. His nose was flattened at the bridge, as though someone had taken a mailed fist to it. His mouth was set, his chin square.

And those eyes. Sweet heaven, those eyes! Fierce and unblinking and as deep a blue as the sea, they regarded Jocelyn with both suspicion and disdain.

"Have you told him what I require of him?" she asked Sir Hugh.

"No. But I have told him that he will not live to see the dawn if he does ill by you." Her faithful castellan hesitated a moment. "He's been hard used, lady. I had a man-at-arms spread unguent on his cuts but Lady Constance should physik them afore they—"

"I thank you, Sir Hugh, but my hurts can be tended to later." Those blue eyes speared into Jocelyn. "First I would know why a Frankish lady must needs purchase a captive to do her bidding. What is this urgent task you require of me?"

"It's a simple matter." Her fists balled inside her long sleeves. "Once it's done, you may leave Fortemur a free man, well horsed and supplied with sword, lance and shield from the castle armory."

He did not leap at the offer. Jocelyn would not have trusted him if he had. She'd developed keen instincts over many years of judging the men and women who served her and her grandfather before her. This one, she'd sensed from the moment he'd stood tall and defiant on the auction block, would break before he'd bend.

Pray God that held true for his oath once given!

"If this matter is as simple as you say," he asked with an inbred wariness she could not but credit, "why don't you set one of your own men to it?"

"I'll explain in a moment. But first I must have your oath that you will never speak of what happens here tonight."

"You would trust the oath of a man you bought for a few pieces of gold?"

"Yes." Only because she had no choice. "Do you so swear?"

His answer came slowly and with great reluctance, but it came. "I do."

A great weight seemed to press on Jocelyn's chest. Her glance shifted to Sir Hugh. He pleaded with her.

"You need not do this," he growled.

"I have no choice." She gathered her courage and her dignity. "Leave us, please."

"My lady..."

"Leave us."

For a moment she thought he would refuse. But he'd served both her and her grandfather for so many years that he finally acquiesced. Not without a final word of warning for the captive, however.

"I'll wait in the guardroom below. One scream, one shout from Lady Jocelyn will signal your death."

She stood silent until the thud of his footsteps on the stairs faded before she closed the tower door. Sir Hugh would see none came up to disturb them, so she didn't turn the key in the lock. When she faced the captive again, she had to struggle to keep the nervousness from her voice.

"How are you called?"

"Simon de Rhys."

"Are you knight or mercenary?"

"Knight. What do you want of me?"

Jocelyn took both her temper and her decisiveness from the grandsire who'd raised her. She'd ordered women flogged and men branded for a variety of crimes without hesitation. Thus she bristled at his tone, yet found herself dancing around his brusque question.

A small, mocking corner of her mind called her a coward. She'd planned this night down to the veriest detail. Had risked her life and those of her escort to set her plan in motion. Yet now that she'd reached the crucial point in her scheme, she found herself hesitating.

"Would you have wine?" she asked, gesturing to the table set close to the stone hearth. "Or dates?"

"No. What do you want of me?"

Very well. He wished it without bard or barding. So be it.

"I want you to lie with me."

He reared back. "What say you?"

"I want you in my bed this night, and this night only. Then you will leave Fortemur with all I promised you."

Brows bleached by the sun to the color of sanded oak snapped together. Suspicion warred with incredulity in his face. "Why?"

"The reason is not your concern," she said haughtily. "Only that I wish to be rid of my maidenhead."

He looked her up and down with an insolence that brought the blood rushing to her cheeks.

"You don't need to purchase a stud for that. One of your men-at-arms could do the deed for you. Or any crone with a broomstick, for that matter."

The crude suggestion brought her chin up. Crows would peck out her eyes before she would admit she'd considered both such desperate courses! But if asked—when asked by the king—she must be able to swear by all she held holy that she'd lain with a man and was no longer virgin.

When that happened, she fully expected Baldwin to unleash the full fury of his wrath. Although he was but a few years older than Jocelyn herself, the king clung as tenaciously to his birthright as she did to hers. Whoever thwarted his plans for an alliance with the emir by taking his ward's maidenhead would suffer mightily for it. She would not allow any of the men who served her so loyally to take the blame. That would be hers and hers alone to bear.

"The why and how of this are not your concern, de Rhys. Only the deed itself."

His lip curled. "So you would barter a man's freedom for a rut?"

"You'll have your freedom, whether we rut or not," Jocelyn returned stiffly. "But it will take you at least a year to earn back the price I paid for you. So the choice is yours, de Rhys. One night in my bed, or twelve months as my vassal?"

Twelve months! Simon's gut twisted. Twelve months, and his father would most like be dead of the wasting sickness that had laid him low.

If Gervase de Rhys went to his Maker, would Simon then be free of the pledge binding him to the Knights Templar? Free to win lands of his own? Free to wed, or at least bed for more than a single night, a female such as this one?

It had been months since he'd had a woman. Although he hadn't yet been formally inducted into the ranks of the Knights Templar, he'd prepared himself both mentally and physically for the demands so unique to their order.

The great keeps that the Templars held here and in the West served as both monasteries and cavalry barracks. Within them, the members of the order lived as pious monks shed of all but the humblest robes and sandals. When called to war, however, they took up sword and shield and faced death with indifference. They were the first to attack, the last to retreat. And whether at prayer or at war, they sought at all times to rise above the sins of the flesh.

Simon knew he would have to struggle mightily with that. He was a man, after all. One with strong appetites.

And the lady of Fortemur was much a woman, he acknowledged. That silken hair. Those ripe lips. The strong, firm chin now raised to such a stubborn angle.

Lust for her rose in him, so fast and fierce it seared his veins. Or mayhap it was pain that licked at his back like tongues of flame. The source of the heat didn't matter. Whatever the reason for it, Simon wanted to give this pale-haired witch what she asked from him.

The man in him ached to tear her laces and strip away her gown. To bare her breasts and belly and flanks to the firelight. Drag her down to the carpet and thrust into her with all the fury that had built in him since his capture.

He wanted her, but he would not have her.

"I cannot bed you, lady, this night or any other. I am pledged to the Church."

"The Church!"

The color bled from her cheeks. Dismay filled her

eyes. Gasping, she dropped to her knees and made the sign of the cross. Once, twice, in quick succession.

"Forgive me, Father! I did not know… I could not know…"

Shame suffused her face and voice. Head bowed, she addressed him in a voice rife with mortification.

"Are you Templar or Hospitaller or parish priest come on pilgrimage?"

Simon couldn't lie, but the truth tasted like gall on his lips. "I am none of those. Yet."

Her head came up. "How say you?"

"I am pledged to the Knights of the Temple, but there wasn't time for my induction before I took ship."

Her eyes narrowed. "So you're still an aspirant? Not bound by the rules of the order?"

"I've chosen to live by those rules until such time as I wear the cross."

"But you're not bound?" She gathered her skirts in both hands and pushed to her feet. "Say me no lie, Simon de Rhys. Are you bound or not?"

"No."

Her head went back. Her nostrils flared. Determination and what looked like desperation darkened her cinnamon-colored eyes.

"Then you need me now even more than before. To be accepted as a Knight of the Temple, you must supply your own armor, warhorse and riding mount along with a squire to see to your needs and mules to transport your equipment."

"I'm well aware of the requirements," he replied, his jaw tight.

He'd brought all that and more aboard the ship transporting him to Outremer. But his squire had been swept overboard during the fierce storm that had claimed more than a dozen other desperate pilgrims. Then, just days later, the accursed corsairs had attacked. Simon had battled ferociously until their sheer numbers had overwhelmed him and he'd gone down, struck from behind by a mace. When he'd awoken, he'd been in chains. His sword and the mail surcoat he'd had forged to fit him were gone, of course. And God alone knew who now rode the magnificent warhorse he'd won in the lists.

The loss of his squire and mount had eaten at him almost as much as the loss of his freedom. Yet none of those disasters could presage the devil's choice this slender, pale-haired siren now offered him.

"The decision is yours," she said stonily. "Lie with me this night and I will supply all you need to join the ranks of the Templars. Or you may serve me here at Fortemur until you've repaid the cost of your purchase."

As he had but hours ago at the swaying rope bridge, he faced a choice between two rocky, untried paths. He could take this woman, as he now wanted most fiercely to do so and leave on the morrow to fulfill his father's vow. Or he could serve her for a year or more, let his father rot away and put his own soul at risk.

His eyes cold and his heart like flint, Simon made his choice. "Remove your robes."

Chapter Three

Jocelyn's throat went as dry as the deserts crossed by the endless caravans bringing silks and spices from Eastern lands. This cold edict had formed no part of her careful plan.

She'd thought… Assumed…

What? That he would drag open the heavy bed curtains, tumble her to the silken coverlet and lift her skirts? That it would be quickly done, and quickly put behind her?

She had not reasoned this enforced mating through, she now realized. Obviously, it would require some effort on her part that she had not anticipated.

Frowning, she cast back through her mind. She might be a virgin, but many of her ladies were wedded. She'd also overheard more than one giggling maid whispering to another. Such frank and often ribald talk of what one must sometimes do to bring a bedmate to hardness now burned in Jocelyn's mind.

Apparently this one needed to see her naked to stiffen his lance. So be it. Naked she would get. Yet as she unwound the linen band that framed her face, her nerves were all ajangle and she could scarce draw breath.

One night, she reminded herself fiercely. One night with this man was a hundred times, nay, ten thousand times better than a lifetime walled up with bored, idle women. Women who, if the rumors were true, must needs pleasure themselves since they so rarely went to their lord's bed. Still, her hand trembled as she laid the linen headband atop the chest that held her folded gowns.

He watched her. Eyes hard, arms crossed against his chest, he followed her every move. As though she were on the auction block this time, to be stripped and displayed for his approval.

"Continue."

She would not flush or cower like a timid maid. She would not!

Gritting her teeth, Jocelyn removed the girdle belted low across her hips. Her keys and the various accoutrements attached to the belt clinked against each other, the only sounds in the taut silence other than the crackle of the fire.

Her heart hammered as she reached for the ties that held her bliaut at the sides. Her ladies usually disrobed her. She wasn't used to contorting like a traveling juggler to reach the laces. Thankfully, the first set gave easily enough. Her rose-hued outer robe gaped on that side, displaying the fine linen tunic she wore beneath. But her fumbling fingers couldn't work the ribbons on the other side. They knotted and drew tighter rather than looser. Lifting her arm, she thrust aside her long sleeve for a better view and pulled on the stubborn strings. They would not give.

Sweet mother of…!

Frustrated and filled with a growing trepidation she refused to acknowledge, Jocelyn was forced to raise her head and meet de Rhys's unyielding stare.

"The strings are knotted. I cannot loose them."

He closed the distance between them. His eyes never left her face as he hooked two fingers in the finely woven ribbons. One hard tug ripped them apart. And ripped, as well, the costly fabric they secured.

Jocelyn's nervousness fled, and years of absolute authority as the chatelaine of Fortemur rushed to the fore. "This gown is made of pail loomed in Alexandria," she cried angrily. "It's worth more than a warhorse, or sword of the finest Toledo steel. You will treat it, and me, with respect or I will—"

"You will what?" he cut in with a swift, tight smile she did not like in the least. "Shout out to Sir Hugh? Have me stretched on the rack? Broken on the wheel? How then will you forfeit your maiden's shield?"

His disrespect fired her fury. Were she not in such desperate straits she would most definitely see him racked. She'd gone this far, however, and by the bones of Saint Catherine, she would have done with this deed and with this man!

With fire in her heart, Jocelyn stepped back, tugged the torn bliaut over her head, and threw it to the floor. Her under-tunic fastened at the neck with buttons of shimmering pearl. They came free of their loops without resistance, and the soft pleats fell to her feet. Shoulders back, head high, she stood before him clad only in her thin linen bellyband, silk-stockings gartered just below her knees and the curved-toe slippers so in fashion at the moment.

Jocelyn was not vain. She knew her breasts were smaller and her hips less rounded when measured against some of her ladies. Nor did she possess the pale, almost bloodless complexion so prized by the women who journeyed to Outremer from the West. Despite potions, gloves and veils, the East's blazing sun had tinted her face and hands to warmest ivory.

Yet troubadours had composed songs to the luster of her pale tresses and more than one knight had compared her lips to the ripest cherries. Many more had begged to carry her token in the lists, although she knew well their ardor was more for her inheritance than her person.

Still, she was not without wit and a modicum of female attributes. So never, ever had she imagined that a man seeing her disrobed would stand like a stone obelisk and regard her with such seeming disinterest!

"Your shoes and stockings," he said in a voice as hard as flint. "Remove them, too."

She did, so furious with him now that she was able to ignore the stinging embarrassment of being forced to bend and display her bottom cheeks.

Heat seared her face when she straightened. It flamed even hotter when he looked her up and down again, as if appraising a mare led into the stable yard for a stallion to mount.

And like a skittish mare, she quivered under his unrelenting gaze. Despite the warmth from the fire, enough drafts slipped past the tapestries covering the walls to cause shivers to ripple across her skin and her nipples to pucker. She could feel them growing tight, see how they drew—and held—his gaze. When those piercing blue eyes met hers again, they were no longer so cold and flat.

"Now me."

The abrupt command made her blink. "What say you?"

"Remove my clothing."

Her jaw dropped, then snapped shut again. Enough of this! She was no serf, no scullery maid, to be treated so.

"Remove it yourself."

He shrugged aside her flash of temper. "You wish

me to service you, lady? Then you must use your hands on me. And your mouth. And whatever else I so desire."

"It takes all that to make you stiffen?"

Something sparked in his blue eyes. Surprise? Derision? Or was it some jest only he understood?

"Fear not, lady," he drawled. "I am as stiff as a lance even now. But if we're to do this, I would have some pleasure of it...and of you."

"Pleasure was not part of our bargain."

"Not part of yours, mayhap. It figures large in mine." He beckoned her forward. "You may begin."

For the life of her, Jocelyn couldn't understand how he'd turned the tables on her. He was the bound servant, she the mistress. Yet now, apparently, she must needs strip the dolt to his skin if he was to perform as she needed him to.

With a thunderous scowl, she stepped forward and reached for the unadorned leather belt Sir Hugh had obtained for him. It came off easily, but she had to work to remove the coarse wool tunic.

Heavens but he was tall! Nor would he bend to make her task easier. To drag the tunic over his head, she had to go up on her toes and press close to his chest.

So close the tips of her breasts brushed against him. The springy gold hair that arrowed from his chest to the drawstring of his breeks made her nipples tighten even more. Jocelyn near gasped at the sensation that streaked from her breasts to her belly.

She clenched her teeth, refusing to let him see how he'd affected her, and stared at an array of old scars standing white against his tanned skin. One angled across his left shoulder, another circled his lower ribs. Battle scars, or gained in tourney. Her grandfather had collected as many or more.

"Continue," he instructed, jerking her from contemplation of his chest.

She had to go down on her knees to remove his borrowed felt shoes and woolen stockings. That put her at eye level with his hips, and the bulge in his breeks gave her ample evidence of the truth of his assertion. He was indeed as hard and stiff as a lance.

Jocelyn's throat went tight. Her stomach tied in knots, and a sudden damp heat swirled between her thighs. Breathing through flared nostrils, she forced herself to rise and stand before him.

"You are not finished, lady."

She could not mistake the glint in his eyes this time. It was indeed derision, with more than a hint of mockery.

Her temper rising, she tugged the strings of his breeks so hard they broke. The loose-fitting drawers gave way, baring lean flanks and thighs corded with muscle.

And his shaft. God help her, his shaft! It was of

a size to match the rest of him. Thick and long and blue-veined, it jutted from a nest of dark gold hair.

"You're too big," she gasped, backing away. "You'll... You'll split me asunder."

Simon's breath hissed out. The unmistakable fright in her voice pierced through the lust her rosy nipples and sleek flanks stirred in him.

She was a maid, he reminded himself savagely. She couldn't know how a woman stretched and grew moist to ease a man's passage. Nor how to angle her hips to take his full length. Now he would have to teach her.

With an effort of will, he fought the urge to drag her down to the thick carpet and take her without regard to her fear or comfort. The fierce struggle locked his jaw and put a harsh rasp in his voice.

"You will not split, although you will feel some pain when I pierce your shield. Surely the other women here at Fortemur have spoken to you of that."

"Yes, but..." Her horrified gaze remained fixed on his shaft. "But they can't have been pierced by one such as you!"

Despite the dizzying combination of pain and lust that held him in its maw, Simon had to smile. "When you are more well used, lady, you will know such a remark strokes a man's pride most mightily."

Her gaze whipped to his face. "I give not a brass penny for your pride! All I want—" She stopped.

Drawing in a shuddering breath she squared her shoulders. "All I want is to finish this damnable business."

She looked so much like a sacrificial victim about to go to the stake that Simon couldn't help himself. His smile widened into a wicked grin. Bowing as low as his as yet-unhealed wounds would allow, he swung an arm toward the carved wooden bed.

"Then get you between the sheets, lady, and we will see it done."

He followed her across the solar. Pleasure warred with pain as his hungry gaze roamed from her unbound hair to her swaying hips to her trim calves and shapely ankles. When he made the return trip, his eyes fixed on the linen band swathing her hips.

Did she have her monthly courses? Is that why she bound herself? It wouldn't matter to Simon if that were the case, although he knew most women shied away from intimacy at such a time. But he saw no thickened cloth within the band that would indicate such was the case with the Lady Jocelyn.

Mayhap this was some new fashion. Some trick learned from Eastern women to entice their men. If so, it most certainly worked. The promise of the shadowed cleft between her rear cheeks put him in a sweat.

Stiff-spined, she drew back the heavy bed curtains. They rattled on their iron rings like the chains he'd worn but a short time ago. The sound was loud in his ears as she dragged down an exquisitely embroidered coverlet. When she slid onto the linen sheets, the down-filled mattress rustled beneath her and gave off the sweet scent of rosemary and lavender. She lay there, rigid and unmoving, while Simon looked his fill. Her breasts were high and proud and pink tipped, her waist narrow, and her mound…

His groin tightened, so hard and fast he near doubled over. He hadn't thought the woman could make him hurt more than he already did, but the pale gold curls at the apex of her thighs had him gritting his teeth.

"Move to the side and give me room."

She paled at his gruff tone, and Simon swallowed a curse. Oaf that he was, he'd only added to the woman's fear. He would have to work now to make sure she could indeed take him. Pray God and all the saints he didn't spill himself in the process.

He managed to hold back, but the urge to thrust into her was like a knife in his belly. Each stroke of his hand, every brush of his mouth on her heated skin drove the blade deeper. And when he suckled first one breast, then the other, her gasp of surprised pleasure came within a hairbreadth of shattering his iron control.

Her scent filled him. Musk from the golden pomander she'd worn on her girdle. Costly scented oil brushed into her silken tresses. Rosemary and lavender from her bed. And female. Hot, sensual female.

He was afire front and back when he kneed her legs apart. Taut as a bowstring when he slid his palm down the quivering curve of her stomach to cup her mound. Levering onto his elbow, he watched her face as he spread her slick folds and thumbed the nub at her center.

The eyes she'd squeezed shut flew open. A flush spread across her cheeks. When he pressed the nub, she bit down on her lower lip but couldn't hold back the small, breathless pants that escaped her. Nor the wet heat that dampened Simon's hand. But when he slid a finger inside her, she bucked and tried to scuttle away.

He restrained her easily. "Let me pleasure you. It will ease our joining."

His words came low and gruff and hoarse. He felt as though he were on the rack. His back flamed, and his groin ached with such savagery he could scarce draw breath. It took all he had to contain his own vicious need and slide his finger in, out, and in again.

When he judged her ready, he kneed her legs farther apart and positioned himself between her thighs. He rested his weight on a bent arm. With his free hand, he guided his shaft to her hot, slick flesh.

The tip probed, pushed, entered. She gasped again and wiggled frantically.

"Wait, de Rhys! Wait! It's too monstrous! You cannot... I cannot..."

"Aye, sweeting, we can."

He canted his hips until the tip was well and truly lodged, then bent again to suckle. His teeth rasped the tight, hard nipple. His tongue soothed it. When she gave a hoarse moan and thrashed her head back and forth on the bolster, Simon knew she could take his full length. Straightening, he flexed his thighs and thrust home.

Jocelyn gave a mewling cry and arched under him. The pain she'd been warned to expect came sharp and fast, but lasted only a few moments. With his second and third thrust, she began to feel something almost pleasurable.

As the feeling gathered intensity, her breath grew short and hot. Her senses whirled. Blind instinct led her to hook her calves around his and lift her hips to meet his. But just when she thought the sensations gathering low in her belly would lead to something more, something that beckoned tantalizingly just beyond her reach, he lunged a final time.

Grunting, he collapsed atop her and buried his face in her neck. She waited, scarce daring to breathe. Her heart hammered in her chest. Her nerves sizzled and spit like hot coals.

Yet he made no further move. None at all. Except for the rise and fall of the chest mashing hers and a raspy rustle of his breath in her ear, she might have thought him dead.

Slowly, so slowly, the fire in her blood subsided. Pressed into the mattress by de Rhys's slack body, she became all too aware of his weight. The man was as heavy as an ox. Her nose wrinkled as she breathed in his sweat-drenched scent. And the odor of the sticky wetness that now trickled between her legs.

So much for the sly grins and titillated laughter of her ladies, she thought in chagrin. This business of mating was all well and good enough in its way, but…

Somehow Jocelyn had expected more. Oh, her body had heated everywhere de Rhys had stroked it. And she'd near come out of her skin when he'd tormented her breasts. Yet all this fuss and bother had left her wanting. Not to mention smelly and sweaty and thoroughly disgruntled.

And now the dolt came close to smothering her. Scowling, she pushed at his shoulder. "De Rhys. You're too heavy by half. Move yourself."

He made an inarticulate sound and rolled onto his back. "Sorry, sweeting."

That was another matter, she thought in mounting frustration. That casual endearment, as if she was some slattern he'd just taken out behind the stables. Who was he to address her with such familiarity?

The irony of that thought didn't strike her until she'd drawn the coverlet up to her chin. She'd yielded her maidenhead to this man, had committed the sin of fornication with him, yet she hadn't so much as given him leave to address her by name.

Ah, well. It was done. Now all she had to do was send him on his way. Clutching the coverlet, Jocelyn propped herself up on one elbow. He lay sprawled on his back beside her with his eyes closed and one knee bent. The gold hair dusting his chest glinted in the firelight.

And, she saw with a gulp, the shaft that had so unnerved her with its jutting size now lay limp against his thigh.

"De Rhys," she said again, dragging her gaze from his nether parts. "Gather your garments and dress. You must leave my chamber."

He answered with a low grunt.

"Heed me," she commanded. "You've fulfilled your part of our bargain. Sir Hugh will see you outfitted as I promised. You are free to leave Fortemur on the morrow."

His chest rose and fell in a slow, soughing breath.

"De Rhys! Do you hear me?"

His eyes opened. They lacked their previous intensity, Jocelyn saw with some surprise. Dull, almost lackluster, they fixed on her face.

"I hear you," he muttered.

Was this what coupling did to a man? Drain him of all strength and vitality? If so, it was no wonder knights refrained from lying with a woman before tourneys.

"Then get you gone from my bed," Jocelyn ordered. "And remember your pledge to say nothing of what happened here tonight."

"Why are you so worried that I will speak of what happened between us?" he asked as he slowly pushed himself up. "Do you fear no man will take you to wife if he knows you won't bring him the gift of your maidenhead?"

"I'll bring him Fortemur," she answered, shrugging. "With such a rich dowry, there will be men aplenty who'll take me to wife."

Just not the man the king wanted to give her to. Or so Jocelyn prayed.

"You must go," she insisted. "I would not have my ladies find you in my chamber come morning."

His movements slow and lethargic, he threw aside the sheet. Jocelyn's gaze went instantly to the red splotches on the linen. The stains brought home the full enormity of what she'd done.

"By all the saints..." she murmured.

Then she looked up and another, far more emphatic exclamation threatened to burst from her.

"Holy Mother! What did they do to you?"

The cuts crisscrossed his entire back, deeper and more vicious than any she'd ever seen. Unlike the scars on his chest, these were fresh. Some had scabbed over, some were barely crusted. Others oozed beneath the unguent she belatedly remembered Sir Hugh saying he'd had smeared on them.

Jocelyn had put men to the whip before. Women, too, when their crime warranted. Not very often, thank the Lord, but enough times to know no ordinary leather thong would score the flesh like this.

She scrambled up on her knees, still clutching the coverlet in tight fists. "What manner of lash did they use on you?"

His shoulders rose in a shrug. "One barbed with lead tips."

"But why? And why so many strokes?"

A dry note crept into his voice. "I've been told I have a somewhat stubborn nature."

Like hers, she acknowledged silently while he pushed off the bed with obvious effort. When he crossed to the clothing they'd left in a heap, Jocelyn couldn't take her eyes from the horrific cuts. Thus she saw him stagger as he bent to pick up his breeks. He threw out a hand to steady himself, but found nothing to grasp.

She leaped out of bed to rush to his aid. Before she could reach him, he toppled like a felled oak.

Chapter Four

"De Rhys! De Rhys, do you hear me?"

Her tangled hair falling in her face, Jocelyn dropped to her knees and struggled to turn the man over. It was like pushing at rock.

"De Rhys!"

His only response was an inarticulate grunt.

This was most assuredly not part of the plan.

Cursing, Jocelyn threw on her torn bliaut and rushed to the tower door. A swift descent of the narrow, winding stairs brought her to the guardroom directly below her bedchamber. The three men rattling dice glanced up in surprise at her sudden appearance.

Her disheveled state generated no little surprise. The two guardsmen gaped in astonishment. Sir Hugh kicked aside his three-legged stool and hurried to her side.

"What's amiss, lady?"

"De Rhys."

"What has that whoreson done?" His hand went to the hilt of his dagger. His eyes raked her hurriedly clothed person. "Did he give you hurt?"

"No, but I fear I've hurt him. Most grievously."

"You had to fight him?" His voice was low and fierce and for her ears only. "Why didn't you call out?"

"No, no. It wasn't that." She gave the two guardsmen a quick glance and kept her response as cryptic as she could. "He, uh, sapped his strength such that his wounds overcame him."

Her castellan swore under his breath. "I feared something like this when I saw his back."

A layer of guilt piled on top of Jocelyn's churning emotions. Hugh had indeed told her de Rhys had been hard used. But she'd been so determined to go forward with her scheme that she'd ignored the warning.

"Come and help me with him."

Gathering her skirts, she hurried back up the winding tower stairs. Hugh issued a curt order to the other men to remain where they were and followed. When they reentered her chamber, de Rhys still lay where he'd fallen, his naked body sprawled atop his scattered clothing.

"He's too heavy for me alone," Hugh muttered.

"I'll need to summon aid to carry him from your chamber."

"I can't have him seen unclothed like this! Help me draw on his breeks, then we'll drag him to the bed."

Hugh's glance cut from the fallen knight to Jocelyn. "Your bed?"

"Yes."

She struggled to gather her scattered wits. Her original plan had called for de Rhys to depart her chamber when he'd done what she'd required of him and spend the rest of the night in the great hall with her other knights before departing on the morrow. Now…

Now she must needs cover what they'd done here to protect him from the curiosity of her people and, ultimately, the king's wrath.

"I'll…I'll say I had you bring him to my solar so I might speak with him about his capture," she got out, hastily revising her plan. "While we were speaking, de Rhys appeared most weak. I bade him show me his wounds and was so appalled by them that I insisted he lie abed that I might tend him. That's what… That's what any chatelaine would do," she finished lamely.

Sir Hugh grunted, but didn't gainsay her. Muttering under his breath, he knelt beside de Rhys and pulled the man's breeks up one leg, then the other.

With another grunt, he rolled the man over. Once his nether parts were covered, he signaled to Jocelyn.

"Grasp his arm."

They dragged him to the bed without too much difficulty. Getting him into it was another matter altogether. As strong as Sir Hugh was, he had to strain to lift de Rhys's dead weight. He got him to the edge of the mattress finally and let him collapse face-down into the linen sheets.

The stained linen sheets. Hugh's sharp glance took in the reddish smears and cut to Jocelyn. "So it's done?"

"It's done."

He nodded once, a quick jerk of his chin, and maneuvered de Rhys's legs onto the mattress. When the man was fully laid out, the castellan regarded her in the flickering light from the fire.

"Had it been a husband you'd bedded with, you could show these sheets as proof that you came to him a maid."

She was all too aware of that. Aware, as well, that she could not use the sheets as proof of her lost virginity. The king would question whether the stains were the result of her monthly courses. Or whether she'd cut herself. Or sprinkled sheep's blood on the sheets.

She didn't doubt Baldwin would have his personal physician examine her. Perhaps in front of witnesses. The prospect made Jocelyn writhe inside, but she would endure such a humiliation, and gladly, if it turned the Emir of Damascus against marriage to her.

"I'll tell my women the stains are from de Rhys's wounds," she said with another hasty revision to her scheme.

"If you don't want them to know what occurred here this night," Sir Hugh said gruffly, "you'd best wash yourself first. You have the scent of him on you."

In her flustered state, Jocelyn had forgotten the yeasty stickiness between her thighs. She guessed it, too, was tinged with red. And obviously gave off a distinctive scent. That an old and loyal vassal should have to remind her of such an intimate matter brought heat to her cheeks.

"I'll tend to it."

Nodding, he turned to leave.

"Sir Hugh…"

"Yes?"

"Thank you."

His brow creased into deep lines. "I fear you'll be cursing rather than thanking me before this sorry business is done with, milady."

He took the tower stairs again and closed the door behind him. Jocelyn cleansed herself quickly, using scented oils and a linen towel she wadded up with her torn bliaut. She stuffed both in her clothes chest to be disposed of later. Only then did she go to the door and call for her page.

The remaining hours of the night passed in a seemingly endless blur.

To her dismay, de Rhys soon grew feverish. She and Lady Constance, wife to the knight who governed Fortemur's armory and a woman with great knowledge of medicinal herbs, took turns spreading soothing balms on his inflamed back and bathing his sweat-drenched body. At one point he became so flushed that they feared for his life.

Racked with guilt that she'd brought him to such a state, Jocelyn sent for the castle priest. As gentle, elderly Brother Joseph prayed over the sick man, she sank to her knees on her intricately carved prie-dieu. Head bowed, she pressed her palms together so hard that pain shot through her wrists. Yet the prayers that normally fell by rote from her lips wouldn't come.

She'd fornicated with this man. Until she confessed that grievous sin and did penance, how could she ask God's mercy on him or on herself? And until de Rhys was safely away, how could she confess?

Not that Father Joseph would betray her. The gray-haired priest had lived at Fortemur for most of his life. But he, too, was of the Church. If de Rhys muttered something in his delirium, if the good father learned through other means than confession what had occurred here, his conscience might compel him to report the matter through the Church hierarchy to the Grand Master of the Knights of the Temple. The Templars' rules forbade them to so much as speak to a female. Having sexual concourse with one would cost a Templar his habit, his weapons, and his warhorse for a year or more.

Assuming, that is, de Rhys was even accepted into the order. Politics weighed with the Knights Templar as heavily as it did with the Knights Hospitaller here in the East. While both groups owed allegiance only to the Pope, their continued existence in the Latin Kingdom of Jerusalem depended on the survival of the kingdom itself. The Templars' Grand Master would not look favorably on an aspirant who threatened an alliance King Baldwin was determined to secure.

Her fingers locked so tight her knuckles showed white, Jocelyn prayed most heartily for de Rhys's quick recovery and departure from her life.

He quieted enough by dawn's light for her to leave him in Lady Constance's care while she attended Mass and broke her fast in the great hall with the rest of the keep's residents.

Word had already spread of the stranger in their midst. Between the clink of ale cups and clatter of wooden spoons, she caught snippets of the gossip that was life's blood to the more than three hundred souls who resided within Fortemur's massive walls.

Only one dared query her directly on the matter, however.

Red-haired and ruddy-faced Thomas of Beaumont had journeyed to Outremer to share in the riches and booty of a conquered land. He'd yet to win a fief of his own in battle, however, and must needs be content with managing lands belonging to others. A distant cousin of the king, Thomas counted himself lucky to have been given stewardship of Fortemur.

As steward, he had a hand in fiscal and judicial matters. With Jocelyn's close watch, he kept a tally of all revenue-generating activities within the keep and its surrounding farms and orchards. He was also charged with ensuring appropriate levies were paid into the king's coffers. As reimbursement for his services, he took a share of these levies to himself.

Jocelyn had made every effort to accommodate the man and his sharp-nosed wife. She'd assigned them the sunny bower she'd called her own before moving into the lord's chamber. She made sure Sir Thomas accompanied her to the cellars when she had business in the counting room, where the keep's gold and treasures were kept. Likewise when she unlocked the spice room to dole out precious peppercorns or cinnamon sticks to the cooks. He rode with her when she went to inspect the outlying farms and orchards, and dispensed in her name such justice as she decided appropriate.

Yet try as she would, she could not like the man.

He was puffed up with his own consequence and quick to remind everyone within hearing of his kinship to the king. Worse yet, his wife was petty and cruel to those who served her. Jocelyn had spoken to the woman about that more than once. On the last occasion, she'd threatened to take a whip to her if she struck or kicked or pinched another maid so hard as to raise bruises. Thus Jocelyn had to stifle a groan when she saw Sir Thomas and his shrew of a wife already seated at the high table.

Given his exalted position, the steward sat on her left. As castellan, Sir Hugh held place of honor on her right. Sir Guy, husband to Lady Constance, sat next to Hugh. Jocelyn nodded to her loyal vassals and managed a polite smile for the king's cousin.

"Good morrow, Sir Thomas."

"And you, lady."

The steward's wife inclined her head as was due Jocelyn's rank but forebore to speak as a small army of pages scurried to serve them. Since the first meal of the day was the lightest, they offered only thick slices of bread, cold pigeon breast, sardines drenched in olive oil, stewed boar left over from the night before, pears, candied cherries and a plate of the dates so plentiful here in the East.

Sir Thomas waited to scoop up a sardine with a bread crust and pop both in his mouth before fixing his gaze on Jocelyn. "What's this I hear? Did you indeed ride to El-Arish yesterday to purchase a slave?"

"I did."

"God's tooth, lady! El-Arish is on the other side of a border much disputed between my cousin and the Fatamids."

"I'm well aware of that, Sir Thomas."

"Yet you went to the slave market?"

Jocelyn downed a swallow of ale before replying. The story she'd devised to explain her excursion into enemy territory came easily to her lips.

"I heard there was a new batch of Frankish prisoners to go on the block. I felt it my Christian duty to ransom one or more of them if I could."

The king's cousin could hardly argue with that. So many pilgrims and other travelers had been taken by pirates of late that not even the royal treasurer could ransom them all.

"But the one you purchased," he said with a frown. "Did I mishear, or does he indeed lie in your bed?"

"You heard aright," Jocelyn replied coolly. "When we returned from El-Arish yesterday afternoon, I bade Sir Hugh see the poor wretch was fed and bathed, then asked that he be escorted to my chamber. I wanted to know from whence he came and why he'd journeyed to the Holy Land."

"Yes, but—"

She ignored the interruption. "I know you'll be most pleased when I tell you he has vowed to join the Knights Templar. Of all the great warriors who defend your cousin's kingdom, they are the most fierce."

"That is true enough," Sir Thomas was forced to concede.

It was, they both knew, an uneasy alliance at best. Since their humble beginnings as self-appointed protectors of pilgrims, the Order of the Poor Fellow-Soldiers of Christ and of the Temple of Solomon had grown as rich and powerful as the kings of Jerusalem themselves.

Nor did it help that rumors skittered and swirled concerning their founder's insistence that they be allotted quarters abutting the one remaining wall of Solomon's second temple. More than one rumor whispered the Templars had broken through the walls to search the warren of underground tunnels. More still whispered that they'd found the treasures hidden there centuries before, along with that most sacred of all relics, the long-lost Ark of the Covenant.

Jocelyn didn't believe that for a second. No one, least of all the head of a religious order dedicated to serving Christ, would deny the world such a sacred relic. Still, one had to wonder how they'd come so far from their original designation as poor fellow knights. Poor they were most definitely not!

Sir Thomas's persistent and most annoying drone pulled her from her thoughts. "But why is this would-be Templar in your bed?"

Jocelyn laid down her jeweled eating knife and gave him her haughtiest, lady-of-the-manner stare. "He was ill used by the pirates who took him. So ill used that he collapsed at my feet, raging with fever. Lady Constance prepared healing unguents and helped me tend him throughout this long night."

Lips pursed, the steward speared a date and bit into it. Juice spurted from the ripe fruit onto his reddish beard. Unmindful of the dribble, he chewed thoughtfully for a moment.

"The man must be noble born if he's to join the Templars. Did he give you his name?"

"He did. Simon de Rhys."

"Son of Gervase de Rhys?"

"He didn't name his sire."

"Yes, he did." Sir Hugh leaned forward and looked around her. "He said this Gervase de Rhys is indeed his sire. Do you know him?"

"I know of him." The steward's lip curled. "If half the tales told of the man are true, he would trade his honor for the price of a goat." He pointed his eating knife at Jocelyn. "Have a care, lady. Rotten fruit doesn't fall far from the tree."

The warning made her chest squeeze so tight she couldn't breathe. Heaven help her! Had she misread de Rhys's character when she'd assessed him on the auction block? Would he ignore his vow to keep silent and brag to any who would listen about bedding the lady of Fortemur? Mayhap try to make some claim on her or her estate?

As quickly as the panic leaped from her chest to grab her by the throat, she thrust it back down again. Simon de Rhys had shown his true stripes last night. She might have been an untried virgin when he'd entered her chamber, but she was no fool. She knew well he could have used her far more roughly than he had.

True, he'd demeaned her by insisting she remove her robes and his. Also true, he'd looked her up and down in a manner that even now sent heat into her cheeks. Yet his touch had been… Had been…

Tantalizing. Exciting. Inflaming. Especially when he'd stroked her where no other ever had.

Without the least warning, Jocelyn's womb clenched. So hard and tight that her hand fisted around her eating knife. Shocked to her core by the pulsing sensation, she shoved back her chair and rose.

"I must let Lady Constance come down and break her fast. I'll be in my chamber, tending to de Rhys, should you need me."

Simon was sure he dreamed. Those quiet voices. Those soft hands and cool, soothing cloths on his neck and aching back. They couldn't belong to the horror that had been his life since pirates had stormed aboard the ship transporting him to Outremer.

He shifted, rubbing a bristly cheek against linen smelling faintly of musk and lavender. The scent stirred something buried deep in his mind. He had a vague memory of skin imbued with this same costly musk. Warm, silken skin that heated under his hands.

An answering heat rose in him. Hot. Searing. Far closer to pain than pleasure. The voices faded. Darkness claimed him.

"You must drink."

Dragged from the enveloping mists, Simon tried to shut out the nagging voice. It wouldn't be stilled.

"Do not scowl so at me."

A firm hand gripped his neck and tilted his head. Something pressed against his lips.

"Drink."

Irritated, he opened his mouth and near gagged when a noxious brew slid down his throat. When he tried to spit it out, a hand clapped over his lips.

"Drink it, I say!"

He got it down and pried up gritty eyelids to find he was lying on his side, face-to-face with a woman seated on a low stool. She had stern gray eyes and a face that showed lines of age beneath her elegant wimple.

"Who...?"

Lord! Had that hoarse croak come from him? He

dragged his tongue over dry, cracked lips and tried again.

"Who are you?"

"I am Constance, wife to Sir Guy."

That told him nothing.

Where in the name of all the saints was he? Who was this woman, and this Sir Guy she spoke of?

"Swallow the rest of this draught and I will fetch Lady Jocelyn. She wished to know the moment you came to your senses."

Jocelyn. The name pierced Simon's confused haze. His mind formed an instant vision of pink-tipped breasts and soft, creamy skin. His body stirred in response.

Luckily, the woman seated mere inches from him didn't note his involuntary stiffening. She poured the rest of the foul-tasting brew down his throat, set aside the drinking horn, gathered her skirts and rose.

"I'll send for Lady Jocelyn."

"Wait! First tell me..." He scraped his furry tongue across his lips again. "Tell me how long I've slept."

"You've been abed for nigh onto two days and two nights."

When she departed, Simon rolled over. Or tried to. The effort seemed to tear strips of skin from his back. When the waves of pain subsided, he moved more cautiously, inch by slow inch, until he lay on his back.

Frowning, he stared up at the heavy bed curtains

hung from a frame above his head. Of a sudden he could remember them rattling on their iron links as a certain stiff-backed lady tugged them open. Remember, too, the curve of her waist and buttocks below the fall of her hair.

So she wasn't a dream. Lady Jocelyn. Mistress of Fortemur. He'd really bedded her. Not just bedded, he remembered suddenly, but pierced her maiden's shield.

A fierce satisfaction thrust through his whirling thoughts. He'd bedded only one other virgin. He'd been a callow youth of ten or eleven at the time, completely bewitched by a buxom drover's daughter some years older. They'd fumbled in the straw and he'd almost spilled himself before she'd given an impatient huff and straddled his hips.

As best he could recall, the drover's daughter had been a rough and blowzy wench. The woman he'd bedded last night was anything but. As his mind cleared, the details flooded back: of a lady haughty and stubborn and proud. Trim flanks girded by a linen band. Rounded buttocks that had near driven him mad with desire.

To know he was the first man Lady Jocelyn had wrapped her legs around tugged at something deep and fierce and primal in Simon. He might not have a groat to call his own, but she was his. She would be, henceforth, in a way she could never be for another man.

Not that Simon could claim her. Aside from the fact that her station was far above his, he'd sworn never to reveal what had transpired between them last night. More to the point, his thrice-damned father had sentenced him to a life that forbade any further concourse with all women, including the Lady of Fortemur.

The tread of footsteps in the hall wrenched him from his grim thoughts. Teeth gritted, Simon turned his head to the door as two people swept in. His first thought was that the Lady Jocelyn was both more and less beauteous than he remembered. Linen banded her forehead and chin and confined her hair. Her mouth was set, her chin angled to a stubborn and most unbecoming tilt. Yet her gown's square-cut bodice emphasized the swell of her breasts, and the belt clasped loosely around her hips drew his gaze to their graceful curve.

But it was her eyes that caught and held his. The warning in their brown depths was unmistakable. He was to say naught, reveal naught, of what had passed between them.

The unspoken warning rubbed his feathers exactly the wrong way. He'd given his word. Did the woman think he wouldn't keep to it? The thought that she might hold him in as little esteem as the rest of the world held his father made Simon's jaw lock.

"So you are awake at last."

"As you see," he got out in a voice that rustled like dry corn husks.

His gaze went from her to the richly attired lord who'd entered with her. Red-bearded and broad of shoulder, the man regarded Simon with a supercilious air.

"I am Sir Thomas of Beaumont," he announced. "Cousin to King Baldwin and steward of Fortemur until Lady Jocelyn is given in marriage."

Ah! That explained the fierce warning in the lady's eyes. This man was her keeper. He would not be best pleased to know the king's ward had devalued her bride price by rutting with a lowly knight.

The why of it still nagged at Simon. Why had she given herself to him? And why in the name of all the saints was he still in her bed?

Sir Thomas provided the answer. "You took the fever," he announced. "Lady Jocelyn, in the graciousness of her heart, gave you the use of her own bed so she and her ladies might tend to you."

His glance swung to the woman he referred to.

"It was no more than my duty," she said, not quite meeting his eyes. "I would do the same for any who fell in a dead faint at my feet."

By the saints! Was that what had happened? She must think him the veriest weakling to let a few stripes and a touch of fever bring him down.

"I thank you, lady. Now, if you will send a page to aid me, I will dress and rid you of my presence."

He could tell by her expression that she wished him gone with all speed. She could barely disguise her reluctance as she shook her head.

"Lady Constance says you must stay abed another day, mayhap two."

"With all respect to the lady, I will dress and be on my way."

Huffing, Sir Thomas interrupted with a stern rebuke. "For shame, de Rhys! Would you gainsay the one who bought you out of captivity and now offers you such gracious charity? If Lady Jocelyn says you must remain abed, you will do so until she gives you leave to rise."

Chapter Five

Whatever balms the women had spread on Simon's back worked miracles. By the time the cocks crowed at dawn the following morning, his hurts had lessened to a dull ache and the raw cuts had closed enough for Lady Constance to bind them with a soft, clean cloth. The fever coming on top of weeks of deprivation and brutal beatings had left him pitifully weak, however.

A noontide meal of hearty fish stew brimming with onions, carrots and turnips sopped up with thick crusts of bread went far to restoring his strength. Even then the stern-eyed Lady Constance would not allow him to rise. He lay abed, grateful for her ministrations but beginning to feel the itch of restlessness while she and several other women clustered near the window to embroider an altar cloth with costly gold thread.

The other ladies gave him curious, sideways glances. Particularly a thin female with a pinched, ferretlike face. Wife to the steward, Simon gathered from her comments.

"When do you think the king will summon Jocelyn?" she mused as she plied her needle.

"I know not," Simon's nurse returned.

"It must needs be soon," Lady Ferret Face said, answering her own question. "From all accounts, my husband's cousin is most desirous of the alliance she will cement."

Lady Constance flicked a glance in Simon's direction and responded in a quelling tone. "Such matters are not for us to speculate on."

The admonishment stilled the gossip but not his whirling thoughts. The king intended to use the Lady of Fortemur to cement an alliance? With whom? And when? By all that was holy, what coil had she enmeshed him in?

He got no chance to ask her. Her duties, Lady Constance informed him, kept her busy without. Aside from brief appearances to inquire stiffly how he did, he saw little sign of her.

Yet despite his best efforts to direct his thoughts in other directions, the hours of enforced idleness brought Lady Jocelyn constantly to his mind. It didn't help that he was in her bed. Still breathing in the faint scent of her musk. The knight who'd pledged himself to the Church, the same knight who'd promised to forgo all concourse with females wrestled mightily with the man who could think of nothing but the woman he'd fornicated with.

Memories of their brief coupling bedeviled him. The mere thought of her taste, the feel of her skin and hair under his callused hands, made his rod grow hard and caused him to shift restlessly. So restlessly that Lady Constance looked up from her sewing and gave him a sharp glance.

"Do you hurt?"

He did. He most assuredly did. Yet he could hardly confess the source of his pain.

"No, lady. I am but discomforted to put you to the burden of caring for me."

"It's no burden." Her shrewd eyes assessed him. "Another day, mayhap two, and you will be strong enough to sit a horse again."

"I've sustained worse wounds than these," Simon protested, "and stayed in the saddle."

"I doubt it not. Let's see how you do at eventide. If you have the strength, you may come down to the great hall to sup and sleep this night."

His attentive nurse relayed this opinion to Lady Jocelyn when she returned to her bower late in that afternoon. Simon had been half dozing, but her entry brought him full awake. Every part of him, he acknowledged to his profound disgust. She had but to stride through the door and his groin went tight.

Undeniably, she was much a woman. Even with her

cheeks flushed and errant strands of pale blond hair escaping its linen band. She wore a plain, unadorned gown of blue showing mud stains at the hem. He understood the reason for her disorder when Lady Constance asked if she'd just come from the mews.

"I have, indeed."

"How goes the progress with your peregrine? Is he used to his bells yet?"

"He didn't so much as flinch when I tied them to his leg this time. I'll take him out tomorrow afternoon to test his wings."

"You should have de Rhys accompany you. He frets to be back on his feet. If he's as ready to be up and about as he says he is, a short ride would be a good test of his strength before he attempts the journey to Jerusalem."

Simon could tell from the startled glance Jocelyn aimed at him that she'd hoped to be rid of him before tomorrow afternoon.

"I've told him that he might dress and come down to the great hall to sup," Lady Constance continued. "I'll have a pallet made up for him there."

Once again Jocelyn's eyes met Simon's. He saw consternation in their brown depths, and something more. Relief? Desperation to be rid of him?

"I doubt not you will be happy to have the use of your bed again," he said gruffly.

Her bosom rose as she sucked in a swift breath. Did she think he mocked her or made some sly reference to what had occurred within these curtains? It was obvious she did from the way her chin lifted.

"Aye," she said coolly, "I will. Until the supper hour, then."

Scowling, Jocelyn navigated the narrow passageway cut into the walls. A hundred tasks awaited her attention but she craved some moments to herself. Even more, she craved the feel of the stiff breeze coming off the sea on her face.

Still frowning, she pushed through the door that gave onto the ramparts. The guard serving as lookout in the south tower scrambled off his stool.

"M-milady," he stammered, surprised and alarmed by her unexpected presence in this remote corner of the keep. "Is aught amiss?"

"No." She waved him back to his post. "I merely wish a breath of air to clear my head."

She got that and more. The wind whipped her hair and tugged at her sleeves as she leaned her elbows on a square-cut embrasure. Waves crashed and curled against the rock seawall far below, echoing the turbulence in Jocelyn's breast.

What in the name of all the saints ailed her?

She wanted de Rhys gone. Needed him gone. Were it not for his wounds, she would have sent him on his way long before now. Yet the fact that he would soon leave her bed rekindled the vague dissatisfaction that had bedeviled her almost since his arrival.

It had taken her some time to trace its cause. She understood the irritating sensation now, though. It had hit again, just moments ago, when her gaze roamed the expanse of naked chest showing above his linen sheets.

What she felt was unsatiated desire, pure and simple. She knew there was more to this business of coupling than she'd experienced. Her women wouldn't make jokes about it elsewise. Nor would the maidservants giggle and compare this one's skill at lancing to that one's. Moreover, Lady Constance, as the most senior ranking of Jocelyn's ladies-in-waiting, had explained in blunt terms the rapture that could seize a wife were she so fortunate as to have a husband who would take the time to stroke and fondle her breasts, belly and nether parts.

De Rhys had most certainly done that! Jocelyn's breath shortened as she recalled how he'd stroked her intimately. She'd felt the most urgent gathering in her breasts and lower belly. No rapture, though. Only this continual, most annoying sense that she might no longer be a maid, but she was not yet a woman.

Even more maddening was the knowledge that time was fast running out. The king would summon her to Jerusalem any day now. Or come to escort her to her prospective groom. She must needs inform him of her altered state before the marriage contracts were signed and the emir's vassals arrived to take possession of Fortemur.

The very prospect made her stomach roil. Her grandsire had wrested this keep from the infidels during the First Crusade. The idea of bringing it as dower to an unbeliever, even one who proclaimed himself friendly to the Latins, put a sour taste in her mouth.

As her gaze swept the thick walls and high ramparts, resentment teetered perilously close to outright rebellion. She wouldn't be the first great landholder to defy the king and look to her own best interests. Many a lord and baron warred with each other as much as they did with the enemy. And hadn't Baldwin been forced to besiege his own mother in Jerusalem before Melisande had agreed, most reluctantly, to a division of power?

Jocelyn could hold out here. After taking Fortemur so many years ago, her grandsire had added mightily to its defenses. He'd made sure the keep's residents had planted bountiful gardens, built cisterns and dug enough wells to withstand a lengthy siege. She could order the outer gates closed. Flood the inner yard. Keep all comers at bay for a year or more.

And then what? Sooner or later, she would have to either negotiate a truce or surrender unconditionally. If it was the former, she would have caused her people to suffer the deprivation of a siege for naught. If it was the latter, her men would be put to the sword and her women given as booty to whoever the king sent to subdue his rebellious ward.

She could not do that to the people who'd served her and her grandfather so loyally. She had no choice but to bend to the king's will in the matter of a husband. Just not this one. Pray God, not this one.

Sighing, Jocelyn leaned heavily on her elbows and stared down at the sea rolling against the rocks.

When she went to her chamber an hour later she found de Rhys already gone.

"He insisted he was strong enough to leave your chamber," Lady Constance informed her. "I will tell my husband to keep an eye to him this night, and you may judge his fitness to sit a horse when you ride out tomorrow."

Jocelyn nodded, but she felt oddly bereft when she glanced at her now-empty bed. She'd struck a bargain with de Rhys, she told herself sternly. She would hold to it. Yet she could not help wishing... Wondering...

No! She would not imagine his hard, muscled flanks between her thighs again. She would not grow flushed at the memory of his fierce thrusts, nor gasp at this sudden spasm low in her belly. She would not!

Dragging off her muddied gown, she told herself the morrow could not come quickly enough.

It dawned bright and cool, but a disagreement with Sir Thomas over a tax he wanted to levy on the next Assizes Day delayed Jocelyn's proposed expedition.

As a consequence, her temper hung by a thread when she strode outside and descended into the bailey.

Her barb was saddled and waiting, its reins held by the stable master. Her falconer was already mounted with the hooded peregrine perched on his leather-shielded forearm. Her escort was similarly prepared to ride. Although she would remain within sight of Fortemur's towers, she was too rich a prize to go anywhere without suitable protection. The only one not ahorse, she saw with a frown, was Simon de Rhys.

A quick glance told her Sir Guy had provided him a sword, buckler and embossed leather shield from the castle armory. They weren't the finest, nor yet the meanest, she noted. Guy had also assured her that he'd set the castle blacksmith to altering a hooded mail hauberk to fit de Rhys's broad shoulders. The faint chinking sound of a hammer coming from the farrier's shed told Jocelyn the smith was even now adding the necessary links. All that de Rhys lacked, apparently, was a mount.

"Why are you not horsed?" she asked him.

"It appears the dun-colored barb that carried me to Fortemur has gone lame."

"The dun is not the only mount in my stables up to your weight." Her frown deepening, she turned to her stable master. "What of the courser Sir Hugh rides betimes? The sorrel with the white blaze?"

"She's near to foaling, lady."

"Then saddle one of the palfreys. Surely there is one… No, wait."

She took her lower lip between her teeth. She'd promised de Rhys a warhorse. There were a goodly number of well-trained destriers in the stables, but her knights laid claim to all but one.

"Saddle Avenger."

"My lady! You know he'll let no one mount him." His glance cut to de Rhys. "And I'm told Sir Simon is but recently risen from the sickbed. He has not the strength to manage Avenger."

The knight in question stepped forward. "Is Avenger the well-muscled bay in the last stall?"

"He is," Jocelyn replied.

"He looks to be most powerful."

"Not just powerful, but most diligently trained. He was my grandfather's first choice to ride in battle. He'll lead a charge or block it with equal purpose."

It went much against her grain to gift this ragtag knight with the destrier that had carried her grandsire in and out of battle. Such well-trained warhorses were worth their weight in gold. But Avenger sorely needed the hand of one who could control him, and she'd promised de Rhys she would outfit him.

"If you can ride him," she said stiffly, "he's yours."

Satisfaction leaped into his face. "Don't fear, lady. I can ride him."

His utter confidence overrode her doubts. That and the wry glint that crept into his blue eyes.

"In truth, Lady Constance forced so many draughts down my throat that I must needs do something with the energy they've stirred. Even if it means getting tossed on my head a time or two."

Jocelyn barely heard him. Caught by that ghost of a smile, she near gawked at the man. By all the saints! How could something that simple transform him so?

She'd seen him now wearing a half-dozen or more faces. Defiant slave. Distrustful captive. Harsh conspirator who ordered her so coldly to remove her clothes. Wan and pale and drenched in sweat as he thrashed with fever.

This smiling man was a stranger to her. One who caused her heart to flutter inside her rib cage as she nodded to the stable master.

"Saddle Avenger and bring him forth."

The men of her escort dismounted, eager to watch the show. Her falconer kept his seat but nudged his steed some distance away so the snorting and stamping he knew was about to occur didn't fluster the nervous peregrine.

When word spread quickly of what was to take place, other residents of the keep came out to watch as well. Kitchen maids, the lads who slept in the kennels to keep the dogs quiet, the keeper of the bees. Even the laundresses straightened from the great wooden tubs, wiped the suds from their arms and joined the crowd. They knew well that many a man had tried to mount the heavily muscled bay. Many a man had failed.

By the time the stable master led the warhorse from its stall and positioned him next to the mounting block, Jocelyn was near to regretting her impulsive decision. Despite de Rhys's assertions that he was strong enough to mount the destrier, he'd risen from the sickbed only yesterday afternoon.

Was she so anxious to be rid of him that she would let him risk his newly restored strength? Did she feel so guilty about forcing him to her bed that she would gift him with her grandfather's most prized warhorse? Or was it just this itchy, restless and most persistent dissatisfaction that made her half hope he would, indeed, land on his head?

Lips set, she stood with the others while de Rhys set aside his shield and approached the destrier. It had been saddled and caparisoned with a cloth of red and black. The cloth served as both decoration and identification of friend or foe during battle. It covered a padded leather gambeson that would help deflect arrows and spears.

As de Rhys approached, Avenger's nostrils flared. His black eyes flicked from one side to the other, then back to the man now only a few paces away.

De Rhys crooned something in too soft a voice for Jocelyn to hear. She curled her hands into nervous fists, half enthralled, half fearful of the drama she'd set in motion.

The stable master held on to the destrier's reins but kept a respectful distance as Avenger snorted and pawed the dirt with iron-shod hooves. Still singing to him in a soft murmur, de Rhys advanced. When he was close enough, he signaled to the stable master to pass him the reins. He did so gladly and scuttled away.

Then it was only the man and the steed.

De Rhys looped the reins around one wrist and reached out with his other hand. Avenger's head reared up. White showed around his eyes. The watching crowd held its collective breath, and Jocelyn's heart slammed against her ribs so hard she thought it would jump out of her chest. She'd come within a breath of issuing a sharp order to cease and desist, when de Rhys stroked Avenger's muzzle. Once. Twice. Still whispering, still crooning.

Like one entranced, she could not but stare at that strong, battle-scarred hand and remember how it had gentled her in the same manner. Shivers rippled across her skin as de Rhys swung the reins over Avenger's arched neck and stepped onto the mounting block. In the blink of an eye, he'd settled in the saddle.

For long moments no one moved, no one spoke. Jocelyn heard not so much as a peep or a hiss as the crowd waited for the tumult to erupt. When it did not, jaws sagged and eyes popped.

As if unmindful of the gaping crowd, de Rhys signaled for his shield. He looped it over the pommel, then directed the destrier in a slow amble to where Jocelyn stood.

"Shall we ride out and test the feathers on your bird, my lady?"

The gleam in his eyes belied the nonchalance in his voice. He'd done what few men could, and knew it. Jocelyn had to smile in response to his smug self-satisfaction.

"We shall, indeed."

A stiff wind blew off the sea and coursed through the corridor between the inner and outer ramparts. The capricious gusts rustled the leaves of the fruit trees planted between the walls and tossed Jocelyn's hair behind her linen headband. She paid the wind no mind. As her barb clattered over the drawbridge and through the outer gates, her attention alternated between the hooded falcon perched on her leather-clad wrist and the knight riding beside her.

She could not help but admire his seat. He sat easily in the saddle, using muscled thighs and firm hands to guide Avenger instead of spurs. The warhorse responded with a smooth, steady gait. He was as much a warrior as the man who rode him, Jocelyn knew. Her grandfather would be pleased, she thought ruefully—with the match between knight and destrier, mayhap, if not with the shameful bargain she and de Rhys had struck.

She shook aside the lowering thought and deliberately turned her mind instead to the matter at hand. Her destination this morning was the copse of stunted oak perched on a bluff high above the sea. Ordinarily a full hunt with hounds or birds would take her much farther afield. Today she wanted only to test the skills of the creature she'd spent so many hours training.

Some moments later she reined in atop the cliffs she'd climbed and clambered over since childhood. The wind was stronger here, but its bite was more than made up for by the achingly blue sky and lace-tipped waves far below.

"We'll stop here," she told de Rhys.

Nodding, he drew rein beside her. The others of their troop halted as well. Only then did Jocelyn remove the peregrine's hood. She did so slowly, taking care not to startle it and risk losing a chunk of flesh to its sharp, curved beak. Her falconer had bred the bird from one of Fortemur's most rapacious hunters. Once the chick had shed its downy fuzz and grown feathers, it had been removed from the clutch. Jocelyn had painstakingly fed it bits of raw meat by hand so it would become used to her touch, but she was not such a fool as to think it tamed.

For several weeks now, she and her falconer had by turns let it fly at the end of a long tether. Each time they whistled it back to their wrist, they rewarded it with a bit of meat. Several times the tethered peregrine had taken down pigeons released specifically to test its sharp claws and hunting instincts. Today it would shed its leash for the first time.

"That's a fine bird," de Rhys commented as she stroked its blue-gray feathers.

"Yes, it is."

Not as large or as heavy as the gyrfalcons her grandfather had preferred for the hunt but far swifter. When the peregrine folded its wings and dived on prey, it became no more than a blur to the eye. Jocelyn didn't doubt it would provide many a plump pigeon or juicy quail for the table.

Its sharp claws dug into the leather sleeve shielding her wrist and forearm. One handed, she wrapped her reins around the pommel and fumbled a pair of bells from the pouch at her waist. When she'd attached them to the falcon's leg, she crooned to the bird.

"Are you ready to fly?" She sang to it with a soft, caressing voice. "Will you soar high and return to me?"

Watching, listening, Simon almost convinced himself she sang to him as well as to the bird. Much as he'd gentled the magnificent destrier he now rode, she gentled the skittish bird. And with each movement of her hand, Simon could almost swear he felt her fingers on his skin.

She hadn't stroked him when they'd lain together.

Their joining had been too swift and his back too raw to indulge in prolonged touching and tasting. Nor had he brought her to her peak before he'd spilled himself, he recalled ruefully. She'd come close, though. He'd bedded enough women to know that. Regret, sharp and lancing, speared into his belly as he watched her murmur to her bird. Had he another chance, he would take great pains to give her the pleasure she deserved.

But he would not have another chance. He forced himself to accept that stark fact as she released the falcon. It swooped up and around their heads, bells tinkling, as if unsure what to do with its unaccustomed freedom. Then it caught the wind and soared. Its circles gradually widened until it flew over the forest of scrub oak.

When Jocelyn shielded her eyes with a hand and watched it closely, Simon shifted his gaze from the speck of blue in the sky back to her. The breeze tossed the ends of her silky hair and flattened her gown against her breasts. Her lips pursed as she followed the bird, then let loose an excited yelp.

"He's found prey!"

Some creature on the ground must have flushed a covey of spotted quail. Almost the instant they broke through the cover of the stunted oak, the peregrine folded its wings and shot downward like a bolt fired from a crossbow.

Hunter and prey collided in midair. Feathers were

still flying when Lady Jocelyn spurred her mount. The barb leaped forward. Simon and her escort scrambled to follow.

Carrying its catch to the earth, the peregrine disappeared below the tree line. They followed the sound of its bells through the thick underbrush and found it tearing at the quail's breast. Jocelyn whistled sharply. The falcon raised its head. Another piercing whistle had it slowly flapping its wings and returning to perch on her outstretched wrist.

Since Simon was closest to the fallen prey, he dismounted and cut a strip from the bloodied breast. He'd trained enough birds himself to know they must needs be rewarded for a kill. He passed the carcass to the falconer, who stuffed it in his pouch, and the tidbit to a delighted Lady Jocelyn.

"Shall we loose him again," she asked when she'd fed the morsel to her bird, "or return to the keep? I would not have your cuts pain you."

"Lady Constance's potions worked miracles. I don't so much as feel them."

They both knew that for a lie, but in truth Simon's wounds had healed more than he would have believed possible in so short a space of time. He could move now without fire eating at his back and mount with only a brief stab of pain.

"Send your bird aloft," he told the lady.

He had no difficulty keeping up with her and the others. But when the hunt was done and she drew rein again, he was more than willing to accede to her suggestion they dismount and walk along the cliffs.

She passed the peregrine to her falconer to take back to the mews and sent her escort with them. When the sergeant of her guard protested that Sir Hugh would have his head if aught happened to her, she nodded to the keep looming farther along the cliffs.

"We're within shouting distance of the walls."

"But, lady..."

"Go! I would speak with Sir Simon of matters that concern only him and me."

Wondering what she had to say to him, Simon dismounted and tethered Avenger to a bent cypress. He hurried over to help her dismount, but she slid from the saddle with lithe grace.

"Walk with me," she commanded.

They meandered along cliffs carved by centuries of wind and waves. The sea crashed in and swept out of openings cut by its relentless battering. Seabirds nested in rookeries among the crannies.

Simon had never seen such brilliant waters or wild, foaming waves. "Outremer is like no other place I've traveled to," he said with a touch of awe. "It has such barren deserts. Such rich, ripe orchards and turquoise waters."

Lady Jocelyn gave him a quick, sideways glance. "If you can make the descent, I'll show you something even more wondrous."

He eyed the waves crashing against the craggy cliffs. “More wondrous than this?”

“Follow me.”

Before he could protest, she hitched up her skirts and started down an almost indiscernible track cut into the cliffs. His heart near jumped out of his throat when he saw how steep the way was.

“My lady! Have a care!”

“I’ve taken this path a thousand times or more. Just watch where you tread.”

Chapter Six

Simon had faced formidable opponents in the jousts. He'd also battled more enemies in combat than he could count. Yet never could he remember feeling a cold sweat bathe his entire body the way it did when he started down the path cut into the cliffs.

It was narrow and treacherous and steep. Too narrow and treacherous for anything except mayhap a nimble mountain goat. More than once his foot dislodged loose rocks and sent them over the edge. He fully expected to follow them at the next step. He didn't draw a full breath until he scuttled crabwise onto a somewhat wider ledge beside Lady Jocelyn.

His breath whooshed out again when he saw the merriment on her face. It was the first time she'd smiled at him, really smiled. The impact was like a mailed fist to his chest.

"There," she said, her eyes alight. "That wasn't so bad, was it?"

"Not for a sylph like you," he replied with some feeling. "For someone who has feet the size of mine, it was a dance with the devil."

Laughing, she swept an arm toward the opening behind them. "This, then, is akin to a dance with angels."

He hooked a questioning eye, stooped to peer inside the opening and gave an involuntary exclamation.

"By the crown of thorns!"

He'd never seen the like. The shallow cave behind them glistened with what looked like a thousand points of light. They were caused by the sun, he saw, reflecting off salt crystals burnished to blinding purity by the sea.

"This is my own special place," Jocelyn informed him. "I came here often as a child, whenever I could escape my nurse. When the tide is in," she added as she ducked inside, "the cave is flooded. But now, with the tide out and the sun low enough to strike lights off the crystals it's safe and dry."

It was also a place of unimaginable beauty. Simon could only gape as he followed her into the cave. The glare lessened once they were past the opening, but the feeling the crystals evoked was still magical. He had to drag his stunned gaze away to face the Lady Jocelyn.

"I thank you for sharing your place with me."

"You're one of the few I've brought here. Most are afraid to risk the descent."

"With good reason!"

He took another look around before bringing his gaze back to her. The blinding purity of the cave eased much of the strain between them and gave Simon the impetus to speak from the heart.

"I thank you, too, for granting me my freedom."

She looked away. "It's a fair exchange. Your freedom for mine."

This was the first hint she'd given him as to the reason behind their coupling. Simon had formed his own opinion based on the gossipy Lady Ferret Face's comment. He wanted confirmation so he knew how deep a quagmire he now stumbled through.

"Tell me, lady. What drove you to so desperate a deed?"

She shook her head. "I told you that first night. You need not concern yourself with the why or wherefore."

"Tell me."

She set her chin. "It's better...safer...for you to remain in ignorance."

"Safer?"

She couldn't have offered him more insult had she slapped his face in front of the entire keep.

"Don't let the chains I wore when first we met mislead you," he retorted, stung. "I can hold my own against any man in battle."

"In battle mayhap. But can you hold your own against a king's anger?"

She hadn't meant to answer so quickly. Or spill so much. He could see she wished her words back, but he wouldn't let her take them.

"If what we did will inflame royal anger, it's safer by far that you tell me the reason now. I swore I would not speak of what occurred between us and I will not. But I'll be asked about my time at Fortemur. I don't want to say something in ignorance that could endanger you."

She stared at him for long moments, clearly torn.

"Tell me," he insisted.

A sigh slipped through her lips. "It's a common enough tale here in the East, de Rhys."

"Simon."

"What?"

"My name is Simon. I would hear it from your lips."

"It's a common tale in the East, Simon." Shrugging, she seated herself on a low rock. "King Baldwin would seal an alliance by wedding me to the Emir of Damascus."

"The emir?" Having suffered mightily at the hands of his captors, Simon could not believe the king would hand a ward in his keeping to a foreign pasha. "The king would give you to an infidel?"

"I would not be the first Frankish lady so given,"

she replied with more than a touch of bitterness. "More to the point, the alliance would strengthen Baldwin's southern borders against incursions by the Fatamids and allow him to turn his attention to the Turks in the north. That is worth more than coffers of gold or chests of costly myrrh in these troubled times."

Simon stood silent for long moments. As a landless younger son he knew well the importance of an advantageous marriage. At one time, he'd hoped his strength of arm would win him the daughter of a minor baron.

His father's vow had shattered those ambitions. The Church now demanded all he had to give. Yet everything in him rebelled at the idea of this vibrant, alluring female being given to one of the infidels he'd sworn to vanquish.

"If such matches are commonplace here in the East, why...?"

He tried to frame his question in a way that would not sound coarse or common. There was none.

"Why did you lay with me?"

Her expression hardened. She didn't speak for several moments. When she did, it was obvious she chose her words with care.

"The emir is reputed to have most particular tastes."

"How so? Tell me," he insisted when she fell silent again.

"All right!" Goaded, she shoved back the strand of pale gold hair that had escaped its confines. "The emir prefers to take only untried virgins to his bed. Once he's pierced their maiden's shield, he confines them to his harem. From aught I've heard, they never leave it again. Or," she added in a strained voice, "get called back to the nuptial chamber."

God's bones! No wonder she'd resorted to such desperate measures.

Simon had witnessed this woman's strong spirit. Once when she'd crossed the wooden bridge he was sure would collapse under her. Again when she'd set her jaw, removed her robes and bared herself to him. He could no more see her withering away within the walls of a harem than she could herself.

Nor could he see the king acquiescing without question to the demise of his plans for this woman. Simon knew little about Baldwin, the third king by that name. Only the broadest details of his struggle to maintain his kingdom against near overwhelming odds. And those, he suspected shrewdly, had been much exaggerated to rally all Christendom in support of this Second Crusade. He did, however, understand how great heiresses such as the lady of Fortemur became pawns in this matter of strategic alliances.

"You know the king will not believe your claim that you are no longer virgin," he told her gruffly. "He will demand proof."

She swallowed and nodded in bleak acknowledgment.

"I know."

Simon's jaw went tight. He'd be damned to all the fires of hell before he would allow any woman to be subjected to such humiliation on his account.

"I will tell the king what happened between us."

"No!" Her head jerked up. Her eyes went wide. "No, de Rhys. Simon. I don't ask that of you. The king's physicians can confirm that I am no longer a maid. You need not reveal your part in this."

The idea that some foul-breathed physician would spread her innermost folds and slide his fingers into her moist, slick depths made Simon's nostrils flare. He closed the distance between them and grasped her upper arms.

"Think you I am so cowardly?"

"No, I—"

"I will not let you take the king's wrath on your shoulders alone, Lady Jocelyn."

"You must! Else you will not live to join the ranks of the Knights Templar."

His father's vow rose up again and clashed head to head with the notions of chivalry, with which Simon had grown to manhood. Everything in him wanted to shield this woman from the fate awaiting her and from the inevitable consequences of her decision to take him to her bed.

The sheer recklessness of that decision tightened

his grip on her arms. "This is madness, Jocelyn. You're a ward of the king. You can't hope to escape every husband he chooses for you."

"I don't! I wish only to escape this one! And..."

Her breath caught. Her head went back. She stared at him with wide eyes. Simon saw himself reflected in their golden-brown depths.

"And what?" he growled.

She swiped her tongue across her lower lip. Her breath rattled in, out, in again. "And to know some small pleasure before I was given to a husband to use me as he would."

Some small pleasure.

That, in truth, was all Simon had given her. The shame of it burned a hole in his gut even as his gaze dropped from her lips to the long, clean lines of her throat and the proud breasts below.

Brutal honesty compelled him to meet her gaze once more. "I gave you that, lady. To my shame."

She blinked, surprised and unsure whether to take affront. "To your shame?"

"There is more I could give you. Much more."

"I..." Red tinted her cheeks. "I doubt it not."

He hesitated, well aware he was close to committing another grievous sin. He had but to look in her eyes to decide he would do penance later.

"Do you trust me?"

A nervous laugh escaped her. "I took you into my bed, did I not?"

"Then let me pleasure you."

The red in her cheeks flamed to a fiery hue. Anticipating a fierce objection, he laid a finger across her lips.

"You need do naught. Nor will you feel the pain you felt at your breaching. Instead, you will feel what a woman should when a man takes time and care with her."

"I…uh…"

The confused stammer spurred him to bend and replace his hand with his mouth.

"Let me kiss you as you should be kissed," he murmured, moving his lips lightly over hers. "Let me touch you."

She stood so stiff and unmoving, he was sure she would draw back. Then her mouth parted hesitantly, tentatively, and Simon deepened the kiss.

He slid a callused palm under her linen headband to cup her nape. His thumb traced the line of her jaw. Her bones felt so fragile to his touch. Her skin so soft and delicate. Although he knew from watching her ahorse and afoot that she was strong of both body and will, he ached to show her the tenderness she deserved.

Holding her mouth with his, he tugged the headband free and loosed her hair. The feel of it spilling warm and silky over his arm sparked a fire in his veins. The fire grew hotter with each caress, so hot he near savaged her mouth with his before he recalled his purpose. He would show her what could occur between man and woman, he vowed grimly. Bring her to a writhing, sobbing release even if he strangled on his own lust in the process!

He thrust a hand through her hair to anchor her head and used his tongue to invade the inner recesses of her mouth. When she gasped and would have pulled away, he hooked an arm around her waist and drew her tight. Her breasts flattened against his chest. Her hips pressed his loins.

She grasped his forearms, her fingers digging into muscle and sinew. He felt her body tense and cursed himself again for using his strength to curb her when his very intent was to give her pleasure.

He eased his hold at the same moment her tongue met his. Tentatively at first, then with slowly gathering ardor. The taste of her shot like a crossbolt straight through him. All thought of releasing her fled. Widening his stance, he let her explore at will.

The fingers gripping his forearms loosed their fierce hold. Her hands slid up and over his shoulders to lock behind his neck. She was on her toes now, her body taut and quivering against his. The need to have her rose in him, as powerful and insistent as the tide surging below the cliffs. His heart pounded fast and heavy when at last he dragged up his head. The woman in his arms stared at him with flushed cheeks and star-bright eyes.

"By all the saints, lady." His voice gruff, he stroked her lower lip with his thumb. "Your beauty steals my breath away. How many troubadours have sung songs to this face, this mouth?"

Her flush deepened. "Some few," she admitted on a husky note.

"There will be more," he predicted.

Unless she was shut away from all men's eyes, wife to an Eastern potentate.

Would this emir take her now that she was no longer virgin? Jocelyn seemed confident he would not. Simon wasn't as certain. With her lands and such a massive stronghold as dowry, she would be a rich prize for any man whether she came to him intact or not. The possibility she might yet be condemned to a life of enforced idleness and isolation ate at Simon worse than the lead-tipped whips that had scored his back.

This woman was too strong for such a life. Too proud. Too filled with the kind of fire that kindled a man's own. He was most certainly afire as he glanced about the cave.

Centuries of tides washing in and out had worn the floor as smooth as marble. The last had deposited a pile of brownish kelp. Dried now by the sun, it proved soft and springy to the touch when Simon went down on one knee.

Loosening his borrowed sword belt, he let it drop. It clattered down as he drew his tunic over his head and spread the coarse fabric atop the kelp. Then he swiveled on his bent knee to hold out a hand.

"Come, lady. You said you wished to know some small taste of the pleasure a man may give a woman. Let me give it."

Jocelyn's whirling head shouted at her to draw back. To put an end to this madness now, while she still could. She'd taken what she wanted from this man. She needed no more of him.

Yet his taste was on her lips and the hard, unyielding feel of him had set her breasts to aching and her belly to quivering. Her clamoring senses overcame her common sense.

Once more, she vowed as she laid her hand in his. Just once more.

Once, she realized when he'd stretched her out atop his tunic, would not be enough. Not anywhere near enough. She was so hungry for him, so eager for his touch. He had but to bring his mouth to hers to start her breathing fast. To lay his rough palm on her ankle, slide up her skirts and stroke the smooth flesh above her garters to have her quivering with eager anticipation.

She wanted him. Ached for him. Yet he played with her, damn him. Gliding his fingertip over her inner thighs. Brushing his thumb against her most sensitive folds. All the while his tongue danced with hers. She was near panting when his mouth moved lower.

With tongue and teeth he explored the underside of her chin. The heated skin at the base of her throat. The slopes of her breasts above the square neckline of her bliaut. Then his busy, clever hand shoved her skirts up higher and found her linen bellyband. He toyed with the tucked ends before raising his head to examine it in some puzzlement.

"You wore this the night you took me to your bed. Is it an Eastern garment?"

"My..." She gulped in several shuddering breaths. "My nurse bound me thus as a child. It... It gives me some measure of protection from the saddle when I ride."

The soft, sheer linen came nowhere close to the coarse linen trews some ladies of rank wore to shield them while ahorse. Nor did it compare to the cruel iron belts some Western lords were rumored to lock their wives in before departing on crusade. Yet the mere glimpse of the thin linen strip running between Jocelyn's thighs seemed to stir some primitive urge in Simon.

His jaw tightened. His breath got shorter. With a low grunt, he nudged her thighs apart and ripped away the linen.

"What...?" Racked by sudden, staggering sensations, she arched her back. "What are you doing?"

"Showing you but one of the ways a woman may come to pleasure."

De Rhys's mouth came down on hers. Hard. Hot.

Shutting off all protest. While his tongue plundered her mouth, his hands roamed her taut body. Was that the roar of the sea in his ears, or his clamoring blood? He couldn't tell one from the other. Nor did he care. His world, his entire being, had narrowed to the eager, panting woman in his arms.

When he ceased his depredations, Jocelyn almost sobbed with dismay. Her entire body screaming in protest, she opened her eyes to find de Rhys smiling down at her.

"Don't fear, lady. We're not done yet."

She couldn't fathom what he was about when he shifted and grasped her stockinged calf. Still grinning, he draped it over his shoulder. When he did the same with her other leg, Jocelyn flamed with embarrassment. She tried to free her legs and move away, but he stayed her easily.

"Let me taste you, sweeting."

"Simon! This…this must be a grievous sin. You must not… Oooooh!"

Her head thrust back against the wool-covered kelp. Her thighs went as taut as bowstrings. The swirling sensation she'd felt low in her belly the night she'd taken him to her bed gripped her again. But tighter this time. Faster. Like the whirling waterspout she'd once witnessed after a violent storm far out to sea, the vortex carried her up and up and up. So high she thought she would scream from the terrifying intensity of it. Then, without warning, it set her spinning in a spiral of dark, searing pleasure.

Her spine arched. Her womb spasmed. She heard herself give a hoarse shout, or thought she did, while the waves of sensation crested, one atop the other. Then slowly, so slowly, the world righted itself again.

Even after the vortex subsided, it took Jocelyn several moments to gather the courage to open her tight-shut lids. The combination of tenderness and triumph she saw in de Rhys's blue eyes made her smile and lift her hand. Stroking his cheek, she could not but admit the truth.

"That was nothing like I imagined it would be. No wonder my ladies giggle when they whisper of the mindless torture to be had abed."

Her reluctant admission brought a wicked grin to his lips.

"You've tasted but a small portion of that torture. Here, let me stretch out and hold you close while you catch your breath. Then I will show you other ways you may find release."

More? There was more?

Still awash in the aftermath of those incredible sensations, Jocelyn could not imagine anything that would bring her more pleasure than what she'd just experienced. And yet…

She had but to nestle her head on Simon's shoulder. Lay her hand atop his taut stomach. Breathe in the mingled scents of leather and horse and healthy male. She wanted more than the eruption of a waterspout. She wanted this man inside her, as he'd been the night she'd brought him to Fortemur.

No! Not like that hurried joining! This time…

This time what?

The question bedeviled Jocelyn as she turned and buried her face in the warm skin of his neck. What did she want of him? And what could she give him in return for what he'd just given her?

It was blind instinct that had her easing out of his arms. Some deep, female need that brought her up on her knees. Without stopping to question the urge, Jocelyn straddled his thighs.

His lids flew up. A startled question leaped into his eyes. "Do you know what…?"

She stilled his questions the same way he'd stilled hers, by laying a finger on his mouth.

"You've shown me how a man may pleasure a woman. Now…" She slicked her tongue across her lower lip. "Now I would return the favor."

She had to smile at his confounded expression.

"What? Do you think me so dull of wit? So ignorant because I am—" She stopped, breathed deeply and corrected herself. "Because I was a maid? When my ladies talk among themselves, I listen."

"But…"

He made as if to rise. She planted a firm hand on his chest.

"Say me no buts, de Rhys. Lie still and let me return some measure of what you've given me."

The urge that grabbed Jocelyn by the throat went against everything her castle priest preached most earnestly. No man should lie with a woman not his wife. No woman should think lustful thoughts, even about her lord and husband. God forbid they should indulge in unbridled passions. The one purpose, the sole purpose, of concourse between man and wife was to produce a quiverful of children. All else was sin in the eyes of the Lord.

And yet… And yet…

How could this be sin? How could she ache in every part of her as she did for this man? How could she bend to take him in her mouth, without so much as a fleeting care for her immortal soul?

"Ahhhhh."

The groan ripped loose from deep inside Simon. His entire body rigid, he drew in a long, ragged breath before thrusting her away from him. He turned to his side, but not before she'd gotten her first taste of a man.

When he turned back to her, his chest heaved and he glared at her almost angrily. "I'm sorry, Lady Jocelyn. I did not intend to spill myself like that."

"Did you not?" Surprised, she swiped her tongue along her lips. "That was my intention."

The frank admission took everything Simon thought he knew about women and turned it upside down. The well-born ladies of his acquaintance were wont to play the tease, promising with sideways glances and pretty pouts what they had no intention of delivering. Women of the lower orders tended to be more forthright in their sexual desires. But even with them a man must needs exert himself to understand their confusing and often contradictory signals.

This one played no games at all. She spoke her mind and suited deed to thought. She was also brave and strong and true to her word. And well above the touch of a lowborn knight such as he.

That thought sat heavy on Simon's heart as he pushed himself to a sitting position. "You are a woman such as I've never known before."

Lips red and swollen from his kisses turned up at the corners. "Oh, so? And have you known many women?"

His brains might still be addled from what she'd done to him, but he retained enough sense to sidestep that particular bear pit.

"No more than my share, milady."

She gave a disbelieving huff and reached for her shift. When it fluttered down to settle around her hips, she cocked her head and regarded him with a curious look.

"So tell me, Simon de Rhys. Why would one who rises so readily and takes such pleasure of a woman give himself to the Church?"

His first thought was to shrug aside the question.

But she'd shared her secrets with him. He could do no less with her. Still, he had to force himself to tell her what he'd told no other soul, save the saintly Bishop of Clairvaux.

"I did not give myself."

The memory of his last meeting with his gaunt, wasted father rose in his mind. Gervase de Rhys's lips had twisted when he'd laid eyes on the youngest of his sons who didn't bear the label of bastard. There were plenty enough of those, Simon knew. More than his unrepentant sire could count.

Unrepentant, that is, until sickness had laid him low. As his flesh had withered and death had drawn closer with each rattling breath, his sire had felt the weight of his many transgressions pressing on him like an anvil. He'd confessed those sins to a priest, or so he'd said. Done penance and been given absolution. That gave assurance he wouldn't burn forever in the fires of hell, but so black was his past that he must needs take extraordinary measures to lessen his time in purgatory.

He'd sought every indulgence, promised what little he still owned to the Church. He'd promised, as well, his fifth—and last surviving—legitimate son. Simon had ignored his earnest pleas to make good on that oath until the Bishop of Clairvaux had said gently, sorrowfully, that the oath bound him as much as his sire.

The fact that the bishop was Europe's most vocal

and passionate advocate of the Second Crusade only added to his persuasiveness. It was Simon's duty, he'd argued, as it was that of all men of true belief, to ensure the infidels didn't recapture the most holy sites in Christendom.

Simon couldn't tell this woman of the agony of conscience the bishop's words had roused in him. Or how close he'd come to telling his black-hearted sire he could burn in hell. Instead, he boiled the matter down to its nub.

"My father took sick. His physicians told him he would not last the year. So he pledged me, his youngest son, to the Knights Templar as penance for his many sins."

"As penance?" Jocelyn's brown eyes widened. "Surely the Church would not hold you to such a vow!"

"I hold myself."

"You cannot. You must not. You are too much a man to…" Flushing, she broke off and began again. "Listen to me, Simon. My grandfather fought alongside the one who is now Grand Master of Templars on more than one occasion. By all accounts, Bertrand de Tremelay is a wise and learned man. He'll understand that this vow is not of your making."

"It doesn't matter who made it. My father's soul hangs in the balance."

She sat back on her heels, frowning. "Do you truly wish to give your life to the Church?"

"I gave my word."

"Hmm."

Her frown deepened. Lips pursed, she regarded him with troubled eyes. "You must know this is folly. You're placing honor before reason."

"Honor is all I have."

A look of impatience crossed her face. "Why is it that some men put such stock in the notion that a vow once given may never be broken, while others forswear themselves whenever it's convenient?"

"I'm not such a one," Simon said stiffly.

"No?" She couldn't keep the bitterness from her voice. "Wait until you've spent more time in the East. You'll see how often Christian turns against Christian and kings align themselves with their sworn enemies in order to protect their lands and fiefs."

"It's no different in the West." It shamed him to admit the kind of seed he'd sprung from, but her comment drew a reluctant truth from him. "My father is such a one. Always grasping, always ready to forswear his oath and switch allegiances when it suited him. That's not my way."

She regarded him for long moments. "No," she said at last, "I can see it is not. Well then, Simon de Rhys, you've held to your end of our bargain. I will hold to mine. You will leave Fortemur on the morrow fully armed, with my grandsire's warhorse to carry you into battle."

"He's a gift worthy of a king, lady. Worth far more than what you paid for me."

She arched a brow. "What are you saying? A horse is not a fair trade for my maidenhead?"

"No, of course not. But—"

She cut him off with a dismissive wave of one hand. "The deed is done, the bargain struck. Now..." She drew in a long breath. "Now we'd best return to the keep."

He got to his feet and dressed in his borrowed clothing while she gathered hers. When he'd belted on his sword, he reached down to help her up. She put her hand in his and rose. They stood for a moment, each gazing into the other's eyes.

He needed one final taste of her to carry with him, Simon decided. One touch of his mouth to hers. The memory of it must needs last him the rest of his life.

He bent and brushed his lips over hers. When he raised his head again, he had to work to keep his voice steady.

"I will pray that God keeps you safe, lady."

"And I you, Simon."

She drew her hands from his and led the way out of the cave. He followed her up the treacherous path, braced to catch her if she slipped or stumbled. Their mounts waited patiently in the shade of the cypress. Her smaller, swifter barb was near obscured by Avenger's muscled bulk. The warhorse, in turn, was dwarfed by Fortemur's walls.

The massive fortress dominated the view from the cliffs. Within shouting distance, as Jocelyn had said, but worlds away from the sparkling cave that was her own special place. And Simon's now. He knew the hour or so they'd passed there would remain emblazoned in his heart for all the years to come.

He untied the reins of her barb and held it steady while she mounted with the lithe grace he'd come to think of as hers alone. He was about to mount, himself, when a shout rang through the air.

"Lady Jocelyn!"

Simon spun around. His hand went instinctively to his sword hilt, but the page that came running along the cliff's edge wore the red and black of Fortemur.

"Lady Jocelyn," the boy panted when he drew closer. "Sir Hugh sent me to find you."

"Why?" Her glance flew to the ramparts, as if searching for a spiral of smoke or some other signal of disaster. Seeing none, she asked the boy sharply, "What's amiss?"

"Blondin has arrived!"

Chapter Seven

"Blondin!"

Jocelyn's heart took a quick leap. This was all she needed to set the seal on a day she knew she would never forget. Eagerly, she turned to Simon.

"Have you heard of him?"

"No."

"He's well known here in the East. His verses are most lyrical and filled with biting wit."

"Ah! So he's one of the troubadours we spoke of just moments ago?" A smile creased his cheeks. "One who will sing songs to your face?"

The reminder sent heat into her cheeks.

"He spends most of his time at the court of his patron, the Prince of Antioch," she related as they mounted, "and only rarely travels this far south."

When he did, it was an occasion for great laughter and a chance to hear the latest juicy bits of gossip.

"How fortunate that you don't leave until the morrow," she told Simon. "Blondin's visits are always an occasion for everyone to dress in their finest feathers."

Except he had none, she remembered belatedly. Besides his borrowed breeks and coarse wool tunic and the hauberk Sir Guy was even now having altered for him, he possessed no other garments. Not that he would need them when he was inducted into the Knights Templar. Whatever he brought to the order would belong to the order.

But tonight, Jocelyn decided, she would see him clothed as befitted a knight. He rode her grandsire's destrier. He could wear one of his mantles, as well. The idea took hold of her as she and Simon rode through Fortemur's mighty gates. They parted at the stables, since he insisted on currying and feeding Avenger from his own hand so the warhorse would imprint his scent.

As Jocelyn hurried across the bailey, she saw at once that Blondin's unexpected visit had wrought as much excitement as de Rhys's conquest of her grandsire's destrier had earlier that afternoon. Cook fires flamed bright in the kitchen sheds. Geese and boar roasted on spits. Two maids hurried through the garden, pulling up turnips and leeks by the fistful to throw into baskets. Even Lady Constance looked flustered when Jocelyn encountered her on the stairs to the great hall.

"Where in heaven's name have you been?"

"On the cliffs."

"You'll fall to your death there one of these days."

The older woman clicked her tongue in disapproval but was as excited as the rest of the keep's residents. Too excited, thankfully, to comment on Jocelyn's disordered hair and clothing.

"Did you get word that Blondin has arrived?"

"I did."

"He and his assistants are taking wine and meats in the great hall with Sir Thomas and his wife. You'll wish to greet them, I'm sure."

"I do indeed. But first I must tend to another matter."

Lady Constance nodded, clearly preoccupied. "In the meantime, I must see to the puddings and boiled bacon. I ordered two cauldrons fired. The foodstuffs should be cooked in time to use the hot water to wash with before we sup."

Thankful she had such an efficient lady to tend to these chores, Jocelyn slipped down the stairs to the cellars. Even in the heat of summer Fortemur's massive walls kept them cool and dry. Bypassing the locked chambers that stored precious spices and the one holding salted meats, she made for the counting room. It was here she reviewed rents and revenues thrice monthly with Sir Thomas. Here also where she kept the castle's supply of gold beasants and the trunks containing her most precious belongings. The keys to the room were on the ring that hung from her girdle.

One key opened the lock on the door, another the chest where she'd stored those of her grandfather's things she hadn't given away after his death. She knelt beside the chest and stifled a familiar stab of grief.

Sir William had been big and bluff and swift to exact retribution for any crime, be it large or small. Jocelyn had learned the fine art, and often crushing responsibility, of governance at his hand. And from him she'd inherited the absolute determination to hold what was hers.

Her aching grief had dulled in the months since his death, but the pangs sharpened as she lifted the trunk's heavy lid and the costly scent of sandalwood drifted from the carefully folded garments. These had been her grandfather's finest. Some of the robes were trimmed with the fur of lynx or fox, others lavishly embroidered with gold or silver thread.

They were supposed to have gone to her husband as part of her dower. Not that the Emir of Damascus would deign to wear them. They were too heavy for the heat of the desert, and too Frankish in design. So it was only fitting, she thought with a touch of defiance, that she should gift one of these robes to the man she'd taken to her bed in a deliberate and most desperate scheme to avoid being sent to the emir.

She dug deeper into the chest and found the garment she sought. Ironically, the soft, fine wool was dyed a color called Saracen blue—so named for the brilliant skies of the East. The hue matched almost exactly that of Simon de Rhys's eyes. She pulled the robe from the bottom of the pile and held it to her face with both hands. Part of her knew she should be shamed to her depths to kneel here, clutching one of her grandfather's prized garments, and think of the eyes that had skimmed over her naked flesh just hours ago.

Another part shivered with a forbidden thrill. She might never have experienced that thrill if not for Simon de Rhys. She doubted the emir, if she were given to him, would take the time to pleasure a frightened virgin. Or even believe that she should be pleasured. Jocelyn had heard whispers of dire mutilations to suppress all carnal desires. And not just to the eunuchs who served in harems.

That would not be her fate!

It could not!

Shuddering, she dug out a lavishly embroidered undertunic, slammed the trunk's lid, locked it and left the counting room. She hurried up the tower stairs and almost burst out onto the steps that led to the bailey. So precipitate was her ascent that she had to take a deep breath before calling to the gangly youth making his way across the bailey.

"You! Will Farrier!"

The youngest son of her farrier bobbed his head. "Aye, milady?"

"Have you seen the one called Sir Simon?"

"I have, lady. He's in the stable. I just spoke with him," young Will added in his solemn, wide-eyed way. "He says he leaves on the morrow to join the Knights Templar."

"So he does."

"Would that I could go with him!"

His fervency didn't surprise Jocelyn. The Knights Templar had earned their reputation as the foremost and most fearsome warriors in the land. Every young page or squire in training viewed them as models to be emulated on the field of battle. Not all, of course, wished to join them in their Holy Orders.

Jocelyn considered that as she crossed the bailey. She'd intended to consult Sir Hugh about which of the squires in training at Fortemur might act as Simon's squire until he acquired one of his own. Will Farrier might do instead. Quite well, in fact.

The boy was not yet eleven but tall and overly serious for his age. And so very, very devout. He served the castle priest assiduously at morning Mass and sang every Pater Noster and Ave Maria in a high, clear voice that would no doubt change with age. Jocelyn had already discussed with his parents and with Father Joseph sponsoring the lad's entrance as an oblate into one of the monasteries here in the Holy Land when he came of age.

Mayhap he could join the Templars instead. Will hadn't trained for battle, but he had assisted his father at the bellows. He knew how to forge a blade and shoe a horse. Since he was from the lower orders, he could train to become a sergeant. In that capacity, he could care for Simon's weapons and ride into battle at his side.

She would speak to his parents, Jocelyn decided. But first she would—

"By all the saints!"

She stumbled to a dead stop just outside the thatch-roofed stable. The familiar odor of horse sweat and manure filled her nostrils. The sight of Simon stripped to the waist filled every other sense.

He stood beside the horse trough, his muscles rippling as he washed himself with a rag and a handful of the soft, squishy soap the laundresses brewed from mutton fat, wood ash and soda. One of the stable boys balanced precariously on the edge of the wooden trough with a bucket in hand.

At Simon's nod, the lad tipped a bucket over his head. Water sluiced down his chest and wet his breeks, molding them to his powerful flanks.

Jocelyn's fingers tightened on the folded robe she held in her hands. As she stared at the bulge at the jointure of his thighs, the sensations from the crystal cave came sweeping back. The wild joy of it. The glorious licentiousness of it.

Then Simon turned so the stable boy could sluice

his back and every wicked, sinful thought flew out of Jocelyn's head. His stripes were healing, but were still so red and vicious that she wondered how he could bend, much less have been able to service her as he had.

How selfishly she'd used him! How thoughtlessly! The realization shamed her, and made the gift of her grandfather's warhorse and robe seem paltry by comparison. Chagrined, she waited until he turned again and saw her to explain her errand.

"I brought you one of my grandfather's robes," she said with a huskiness she couldn't keep from her voice. "He had not your height, but he was broad of shoulder."

"I thank you for the loan, but—"

"It's not a loan. I gift you with it."

"You've already given me all I need. All I could desire of you," he added slowly.

This wasn't a conversation she wished the stable boy to hear. She sent him a stern glance. "You, lad. Give Sir Simon a cloth to dry himself with and leave us."

The boy scrambled to obey, and Simon used the cloth on his head and torso. Jocelyn followed its sweep over ropy muscle and smooth flesh. Wrenching her gaze from his chest, she shook out the robe so he could see the embroidery decorating the sleeves and hem.

"I set these stitches myself."

He lifted one of the sleeves to inspect the intricate floral design. "They're finely done."

"No, they're not," she countered with a rueful smile. "You don't need to bend the truth with me. I know I have many skills. Putting needle to cloth isn't one of them. But I labored over these stitches for many an hour. They're a mark of the love and respect I bore for my grandfather. I would… I would that you have this robe, Simon, and wear it while yet you may."

That would not be long. When he completed his initiation, he would don the simple robe of a monk. Or, when he rode into battle, a white surcoat emblazoned with a red cross. The realization lay heavy between them as his eyes skimmed over her face.

"Then I thank you, Lady Jocelyn. For this robe, and for all else you've gifted me with."

She nodded and spun on her heel. Moments later she plunged into the frantic bustle of a keep preparing for a lively night's entertainment.

By the time she'd greeted Blondin and his assistants and consulted once more with Lady Constance on preparations for the hastily assembled feast, she barely had time to wash and have the tangles combed from her hair. While one maid hastily rubbed crushed rose petals into her cheeks, another whisked one of Jocelyn's best gowns from the clothes chest and shook out its shimmering folds.

"No! Not the damascene."

She would eat pig slop before she would don the bliaut of costly figured silk, woven on two sides to give it a sheen so special that it was named for the place where it had originated. Tonight she wanted nothing to remind her of Damascus or its emir!

"I'll wear the ruby bliaut."

The gown was sewn from Venetian silk. As soft as a spider's web, it boasted a square neckline cut low over the breasts and sleeves so long they dragged the floor. Beneath it Jocelyn wore a tunic trimmed with cloth of gold that showed at the sides when she walked. A chin band in the same paper-thin gold emphasized the long line of her throat and held back hair her maids brushed to a gleaming shimmer. She topped the headband with a circlet of beaten gold studded with garnets.

As she pirouetted in front of the mirror, Jocelyn tried to convince herself that she hadn't taken such pains with her hair and dress on Simon's account. The effort was fruitless. The moment she entered the great hall, her glance swept its length and breadth until she spotted him.

He was seated at the lower boards, as befitted his rank. And as much as she longed to have him join her at the high table, there he must needs remain. She'd no doubt stirred gossip already by gifting him with her grandfather's robe. She dared not raise Sir

Thomas's brows further by inviting a lowly knight to share the high table.

Lady Constance's efforts had ensured that Fortemur rose to the occasion of a visit by the realm's most renowned troubadour. Silver plates and gem-studded goblets graced the linen-covered high table. Gold saltcellars marched between them. Even the trestle tables where the lower orders ate had been scrubbed free of grease stains and sported precious wax candles instead of bowls of tallow belching their usual brown smoke.

Sir Hugh, Sir Guy and Lady Constance were already in their seats. So were Sir Thomas and his pinch-faced wife. Jocelyn gave an inner sigh. The woman's expression was so set in those dour lines that her cheeks would crack if she ever once smiled.

And who could *not* smile at Blondin's clever verses? After scurrying squires delivered the first course of boar's head with brawn pudding, sugared partridge and venison shank with stewed turnips, the bard strolled the hall. He was a small man, thin and shorter by a head than most of those around him, but richly dressed in the latest fashions. He obviously took great pains with the luxuriant mane of hair that fell in shining brown waves well past his shoulders. Rings decorated the fingers of both hands and the heavy gold chain draped around his neck bespoke the worth in which his patron held him.

But it was his voice that was his most precious

possession. As clear and pure as the song of a lark on a bright spring morning, it soared through the great hall as his so-skilled fingers plucked the strings of his mandolin and his underlings accompanied him on flute and lyre.

His first song was a tribute to the beauty and grace of a duchess who went unnamed. It didn't take long to identify her as the ubiquitous Eleanor of Aquitaine, however. Particularly when Blondin made reference to the queen's supposed affair with her flamboyant, fair-haired uncle.

'Tis said she has a smile
Like the dawn,
Eyes like the doe,
And a heart so large it
Can accommodate not just a king,
But a count.

His sly and most unsubtle emphasis on the word *heart* was not lost on his listeners. The verse drew snorts and guffaws from the men, smothered laughter from the women. The troubadour assumed an innocent air, as if he didn't understand their titters, and strummed another tune.

This one made reference to the Lady of Fortemur. It began with the usual paeans to her hair, her eyes, her wit and beauty. It ended with reference to a certain Eastern potentate who must needs watch his back—and his front parts—should he mishandle a bride whose grandfather taught her how to wield a gelding knife.

Jocelyn joined in the applause when he concluded but was hard pressed to keep her smile in place. Particularly when he leaned an elbow on the table in front of her.

"Your coming marriage is the talk of Antioch, lady."

"Is it?"

"Indeed." His clever fingers played with the strings of his mandolin. "My patron, the prince, discussed it with the king when they were both in Jerusalem for the Feast of St Cyril. From all accounts, Baldwin and his lady mother are most anxious to see this joining done."

Troubadours, wandering minstrels and jongleurs were as eagerly welcomed for the news and gossip they brought as for their entertainment. Jocelyn didn't care for this bit, however. Nor for the comments that followed.

"There are rumblings that more Turks are rallying to this young lion, Saladin. All agree he represents a most dire threat. One our king intends to deal with. First, though, Baldwin must needs secure his western borders. You should expect to go to your nuptial chamber soon."

No one at the table except Sir Hugh could guess

what it cost Jocelyn to lift her shoulders in a careless shrug.

"Women dispose what men compose. Now come, most eloquent and clever poet. Sing us a song of love true and unblemished."

"As you wish, my lady."

He didn't have to dig deep into his repertoire for a much-loved favorite. The tale was as old as time. A fair maid. A brave and handsome knight. Fates that conspired to keep them apart despite every wrenching sacrifice, every heroic effort. It ended with the lament of the hero as he lay dying in his lady's arms.

Your whisper brightens my heart.
Your kiss feeds my soul.
You are the sun that ends my darkness.
I will be faithful to you forever,
In this life and the next.

Jocelyn couldn't keep her glance from drifting to the lower boards. Every ear strained to hear Blondin's song, every eye was on his brightly garbed person. Except Simon's. His gaze lifted and locked with hers.

She was not such a ninny as to think she'd tumbled into love with the man in the space of just a few days. Not the kind of courtly love celebrated in this heart-wrenching song, at any rate. The feelings Simon de Rhys roused in her were too carnal, too hot and eager and impure. Even now she had but to look at him to see him in the stable again, water coursing over his muscled shoulders and trickling down his belly.

And yet…

By all the saints! There was no "yet," she reminded herself fiercely. She was a fool to let her thoughts wander to what could not be.

And even more of a fool to catch her breath when the boards were pushed back, the musicians struck up a lively tune and Simon wove his way to the head table.

"May I partner you in the dance, Lady Jocelyn?"

Sir Thomas's ruddy face turned brick red at such effrontery. His wife sniffed. Lady Constance lifted a brow. Sir Hugh shot dagger looks from his seat. Traditionally, the lady of the keep opened the dance with the most senior of the knights present. Jocelyn knew she courted gossip but pushed back her chair with a sense of recklessness.

"Gladly."

Simon could scarce contain himself while she rounded the end of the high table to join him. He had but to gaze at her, or recall the dreamy look that had crossed her face when the troubadour sang of courtly, unblemished love, to feel the wanting rise up to almost choke him.

He knew he'd crossed the bounds by asking her to

tread the boards with him. A knight who sat so far below the salt had no business approaching a lady as highborn as Jocelyn of Fortemur. Yet he could no more have stopped himself from taking the hand she held out to him than he could have stopped breathing.

A now-familiar knot tightened in his gut as he led her to the center of the hall. It wasn't merely lust this woman stirred in him. He'd passed beyond that. What he felt for her was dangerously close to the hopeless, heedless passion the troubadour had just sung of.

Luckily, the tune was a familiar one and the steps simple enough that he didn't have to fear tripping over his own feet. Not that he could have concentrated on his steps even had he wished to! The Lady Jocelyn dazzled him. Enthralled him. Aroused a hunger at once base and yet as noble as that song.

Had his kisses put that rosy tint in her cheeks? Had he nuzzled the creamy flesh showing above her gown's bodice? Their stolen hours together now seemed like a dream. One he would have to banish—or at least censor—during the years of celibacy ahead.

But for now, for this moment, he could feast his eyes on her glowing face and vibrant beauty. He could breathe in, as well, her delicate scent of musk, colored tonight with a touch of jasmine.

The movement of the steps took them down the line of dancers. At the end of the row, he gripped her waist, lifted her four inches off the floor and swung her in a circle. Laughing, she regained her footing and took his arm while they retraced their way up the line.

"You're surprisingly light on your feet for one so… so…"

"So big?" he supplied with a grin.

"So big. And more than passing handsome in that robe, if I may be so bold as to say so."

"You may, lady."

The smug reply drew another rippling laugh from Jocelyn. The man had a wit about him, she acknowledged. She'd glimpsed it briefly in the cave, when his eyes had taken on a wicked glint. If she hadn't turned her head at that moment, she might have been tempted to tease another such response.

But the expressions on the faces of those watching her so intently killed every impulse to laugh and tease. Thomas was leaning forward, his scowl deep as he followed their every move. His beak-nosed wife was no less attentive. Worse, much worse, Blondin slanted inquisitive glances their way as he strolled the hall. Jocelyn would be hard put to protect Simon from the king's wrath if the troubadour linked de Rhys's name to hers in one of his sly songs.

As soon as the tune ended, she loosed her hand and tipped her head in a gracious nod. "I thank you, Sir Simon. You partner a lady well."

In more than just the dance. The unspoken message lay in the smile she gave him.

"Now, if you'll escort me back to the table, I must signal the pages to bring in the next course."

He complied, then bowed and pressed a kiss on the back of her hand. It was no more than a common courtesy, but Jocelyn felt the heat of his lips burn like a brand. She covered her involuntary shiver well…or thought she did.

Sir Hugh waited until another song had struck up to lean closer and murmur in her ear.

"You'd best have a care, lady. You don't want to show de Rhys too much attention."

"As you say."

"Nor," he added with the candor of a long and faithful advisor, "should you take him again to your special cave. It's not safe, for either of you."

Jocelyn fought the flush that threatened to rise above the neck of her gown. "He leaves on the morrow, Hugh, as soon as we have outfitted him with the accoutrements I promised him."

The castellan grunted and settled back in his chair.

Chapter Eight

The courier arrived shortly after dawn the next morning. He'd ridden through the night and clattered across the drawbridge on a lathered mount. Chickens and swine scattered at his approach. Stable lads scurried to take his reins.

Sir Hugh sent one of the keep's guardsmen to notify Jocelyn. He caught her just as she and Simon were on their way to speak to Will Farrier and his parents about the possibility of young Will becoming Simon's squire.

"A royal courier has arrived, milady!"

The announcement brought Jocelyn's head around with a snap. Her heart seemed to stop dead in her chest before starting again with a painful kick.

"Sir Hugh sent me to find you," the guardsman panted. "He and the courier await you in the keep."

Her stricken gaze flew up to lock with Simon's.

"Mayhap it's not the summons you fear," he said in what she knew he intended as a reassuring tone. "Mayhap the king merely wishes you to send a levy of men-at-arms to counter this threat the troubadour spoke of last night."

"Mayhap," she got out on a ragged note. "Although after the news Blondin brought regarding Saladin, I very much fear otherwise."

Spinning on her heel, she retraced her steps. Simon accompanied her back to the keep. Sir Hugh met them just inside, with Thomas of Beaumont hovering at his elbow.

The king's cousin looked as tense as Jocelyn felt. With good reason, she thought grimly. When she married, her husband would assume control of her estates and Thomas's lucrative stewardship would end. The landless knight would have to throw himself once again on the king's largesse to find another fief to skim monies from.

"Where is the courier?"

"In the great hall. Lady Constance has supplied him with food and ale."

Nodding, Jocelyn hurried past servants still gathering scraps from the morning meal to give to the poor. Sir Hugh fell into step with her. Sir Thomas hurried alongside. She didn't think to address Simon. Her mind was too full, her thoughts too churning with emotion. Yet the sound of his steady tread a few paces behind was oddly reassuring.

Odd, and most absurd. He'd done all she'd demanded of him, Jocelyn reminded herself fiercely. His role in this farcical masque was done. She must needs face what lay ahead alone. The grim realization added a sharp edge to her voice as she addressed the dust-coated courier.

"I am Jocelyn of Fortemur. You have a message for me?"

"Aye, lady."

The courier scrambled to his feet and drew a folded parchment from the leather pouch slung over one shoulder. Her heart thudded at the sight of the seal pressed into the red wax. One large cross with four smaller crosses in each corner. The insignia adopted but recently by King Baldwin III as part of his deliberate campaign to separate himself from his mother's long and very active regency.

Disgusted by the tremble in her hand, Jocelyn took the parchment and broke the seal. Her eyes skimmed the few lines of Latin script. Her breath rattled in, then out again as she read them a second time. Then she lifted her gaze to the others.

"The king has received word that Saladin has made overtures to the Emir of Damascus."

She had to force the words out through a throat gone tight and dry. All her hopes, all her fears, stared her in the face.

"Baldwin..." She struggled for breath. "Baldwin fears the emir may be considering an alliance with Saladin. The king would spike those plans by proceeding with my proposed marriage to Ali ben Haydar forthwith. He instructs me to prepare to travel to Damascus within the fortnight."

"So he would still give you to that thrice-damned despoiler of young virgins!"

Sir Hugh followed his disgusted exclamation with an oath so foul it moved Sir Thomas to protest on his cousin's behalf.

"Why do you curse? The match has been months in the making. It would appear even more urgent now."

Hugh ignored him, his gaze locked with Jocelyn's. "What will you do?"

"Go to Jerusalem at once and explain."

"Explain?" Thomas echoed, frowning. "What is there to explain?"

Jocelyn paid him no heed. Her thoughts were already winging toward all she needed to do to ready for a swift journey.

"I'd best instruct my ladies to pack a trunk."

Sir Hugh nodded. "I'll order your escort and have my mount saddled."

"No!"

She wanted no hint of Sir Hugh's part in her desperate scheme to reach the king's ears. She, and she alone, would bear the consequences of her actions.

"I would that you remain at Fortemur. Sir Thomas will need your wise counsel in my absence."

The self-important steward issued an indignant protest. "I'm well familiar with my duties, lady. I need him not."

"And you require a strong arm to lead your escort," Sir Hugh said. "You'll be forced to spend at least one night on the road, mayhap two. You must have protection."

"Sir Guy can command my escort. Or…"

She paused, and when her gaze shifted to Simon, she knew she'd just made another pact with the devil.

"Simon de Rhys has shown he's well enough to sit a warhorse," she said, ignoring the frowns directed at her by both castellan and steward. "I have no doubt he can swing a sword as well, if need be. Since he, too, must needs travel to Jerusalem, he can captain my guard."

And once they reached the city gates, they would go their separate ways. Jocelyn would not have Simon present when she faced the king any more than she would Sir Hugh.

She kept that thought uppermost in mind as she rushed to fulfill the rest of her bargain. She'd promised him the accoutrements required by a Knight Templar. And, she insisted, he would have them.

While her ladies packed what she would need for the journey, Jocelyn accompanied him and Sir Guy to the castle armory. Luckily, the ironsmith had completed the alterations to a hauberk that would fit Simon's broad shoulders. He'd also had the tanner stitch a leather surcoat to wear over the chain mail so the sun would not blaze down on it and cook its wearer alive.

After they were assured of the fit, Sir Guy provided a helm, lance, battle-ax and mace from those stored on wooden racks within the armory. Then Jocelyn once again turned her attention to the matter of a squire. She sent a page requesting her farrier, his goodwife and their youngest son to the keep. Once they'd arrived, clearly nervous and unsure why they'd been summoned, she laid the choice before them.

"You know I've spoken with Father Joseph regarding Will's wish to go into Holy Orders."

Tom Farrier nodded. The grime of his profession was caked deep in the creases of his face and beneath his nails. His shoulders were as broad as hewn oaks, his arms and thighs heavily roped with muscle. If the son grew to fill the father's shoes, Jocelyn thought, he would do well indeed as a squire.

"I've promised to buy his admittance into an order when he comes of age and so I will. Or," she said slowly, "should he wish it and you agree, I'll outfit him so he may accompany Sir Simon and join the ranks of the Knights Templar as a sergeant when he has proven himself."

"Milady!" Shaking with excitement, the gangly, thatch-haired youth whooped with delight. "I will serve him most faithfully, I swear. If…" He turned an eager, hopeful face to Simon. "If you'll have me."

Simon's keen blue eyes measured him from head to foot. "What do you know of arms, lad?"

"I've worked the bellows for my father this many a year. He's taught me to hone a sword blade to a feather's edge and keep rust from chain mail by oiling it with essence of camellia and clove."

His words spilled out in an excited rush, one atop the other and filled with earnest entreaty.

"I can fletch a crossbow bolt, even a quarrel if necessary. I swear to you, sir, you may trust me with your mace or war ax or halberd or lance…"

Simon held up a hand to interrupt the fervent litany. "And horses? What do you know of them and their barding?"

The lad's face fell. "Not as much as I do of arms and armor," he admitted. "The only horse I've been allowed to ride is the dray my father uses to haul wood for the fires. She moves with the speed of a slug."

His profound disgust had Jocelyn biting her lip to hide a smile. The dray horse was big and powerful but did indeed plop one hoof in front of the other with great deliberation. She said nothing as Will and his parents awaited Simon's decision.

"Well," the knight said after several moments of consideration, "you'll have time to test your seat on something brisker during the journey to Jerusalem."

"You mean...?" Will's eyes blazed with joy and disbelief. "You mean you'll have me?"

"Aye, lad. As long as you understand that I'll work you until your bones ache and you want to weep with weariness." His face set, Simon brushed aside Will's stammering assurances that he understood full well. "Most boys spend years as a page before they become squires. Then they must learn battle tactics and often earn broken bones or bloodied heads before they accompany a knight into the field. You won't have that luxury. You'll need to learn, and learn fast."

"I will, I swear!"

"You'd better. Both our lives depend on it."

Tom Farrier left beaming, his wife alternating between pride and tears. Their son almost skipped out in his impatience to gather his belongings.

With Simon's outfitting in hand, Jocelyn turned her attention to her own. She hurried up to her chamber to find her maids almost done with packing her traveling trunk and that of the lady she'd selected to accompany her on the journey. Lady Beatrix was wife to one of the keep's lesser knights. She had no children as yet, was only a few years older than Jocelyn and could sit a saddle almost as well. She would have no trouble making the hurried journey.

The Lady of Fortemur departed her keep after a rushed noon meal. Half of her eight-man escort rode in the van, the other half to the rear. In between rode two pages, Lady Beatrix, a pack mule with provisions for the journey and another mule bearing the hastily packed trunks.

After conferring with the sergeant of the guard and confirming the order of march, Simon positioned himself at the head of the column. Despite his protest, Jocelyn did the same. She had no desire to eat the dust of the road. Or so she informed him. Yet they both knew the truth. Fate had given them a few more hours together. They were each loath to waste them.

Nor did they.

Once they gained the main coastal road heading north, the going was slow. Merchants and caravaneers plied the busy thoroughfare with long lines of camels or mules strung out behind them. Jocelyn's troop jostled for space with pilgrims of every nation. Some traveled in large companies with armed escorts. Some were afoot and had banded together with two or three others for safety.

Simon remained vigilant at all times, but slowly, albeit reluctantly, satisfied some of the questions Jocelyn still harbored about him.

Bit by bit she learned of his years as page, then squire to a minor baron. And of the battle where the baron had gone down and Simon had deflected the vicious blow that would have decapitated the Duke of Angoulême.

"Henri knighted me right there on the field."

"He must not have put a high value on his life if he didn't give you lands and a title as well as your spurs," Jocelyn commented.

"He might have, had he not taken sick and died less than a week later." Simon's mouth curved in a rueful grin. "Henri was battling his son and heir when I deflected that blow. As a consequence, the new duke was not particularly pleased that I extended his father's life, if only by a few days."

"How did you make your way after that?"

"By hiring out my sword and taking prizes in tourneys."

It was a common practice for younger sons to hire out as mercenaries. Particularly sons whose fathers had left them no patrimony. Intensely curious about the man who had bound his youngest son to a life of celibacy and service to the Church, she probed deeper.

"Tell me of your father. When did he contract the wasting sickness?"

"Six months ago. I took ship for the Holy Land not long after."

"So..." Her breath caught. "So the sickness may have already claimed him?"

A muscle twitched in the side of Simon's jaw. The possibility had occurred to him, too, Jocelyn realized. More often than not.

"Wouldn't his death release you from his vow?"

"Not according to the Bishop of Clairvaux."

The terse reply silenced her for some moments. The saintly bishop's name was as well known here in the East as it was in the West. The Second Crusade was due in great part to his personal efforts.

The Pope himself had commissioned the bishop to recruit Crusaders. At Clairvaux's insistence, he'd granted the same indulgences for this great cause as had been granted in the First Crusade. The bishop had then expounded to such length on the taking of the cross as a means of gaining absolution for sin and attaining grace that he'd been able to incite not just kings and queens, but huge armies of the faithful. After preaching in a field filled with listeners, the entire crowd reportedly enlisted en masse. When cloth merchants ran out of material to make crosses, the bishop was said to have given up his own outer garments so they might fashion more.

That the Second Crusade had so far failed dismally in its objective of reclaiming territory lost to the Saracens in no way detracted from the bishop's renown. Nor, judging by Simon's presence in the Holy Land, from Clairvaux's ability to convince sinners that this was a path to redemption.

"What of your mother?" Jocelyn asked after a moment. "Does she, too, expect you to hold to your father's vow?"

"She died when I was a babe." His voice went hard and cold. "After my sire beat her senseless, I'm told, for ordering stewed rabbit to be served at the high table when he'd specifically desired it roasted."

"My God! And this is the man who forces you to give the remaining years of your life to the Church?"

When her outburst was met with a stony silence, Jocelyn bit back another sharp comment. Who was she to harangue him for holding to his concepts of duty and honor? Firmly suppressing the urge to dissuade him from a course she now considered most misguided, she sought less controversial topics.

She soon discovered he was a wealth of information on diverse topics ranging from political maneuverings to the latest ladies' fashions to the controversy swirling around Eleanor of Aquitaine.

"It's true?" Jocelyn gasped. "The Pope will give her an annulment from Louis of France?"

"So it's rumored, although it was Louis who petitioned for the dissolution of their marriage. Even kings don't like to wear horns apparently."

The reasons behind the annulment went well beyond Eleanor's supposed affair with her uncle, of course. In their fifteen years of marriage, the queen had born Louis two daughters but no son and heir. Moreover, from all accounts the French king was as meek and pious as his wife was strong-willed and worldly.

"It's said she's already planning marriage to Henry

of Anjou," Simon commented. "Soon, if she and Henry have their way, to be king of England."

Envy and an almost choking wish that she could emulate the redoubtable Eleanor imbued Jocelyn's response. "Now there," she said fiercely, "is a woman who rules her own fate."

"She does, indeed."

They rode in silence for a few moments before Jocelyn broke it.

"Eleanor's cousin and supposed lover, Raymond, fell in the battle for Inab, and the infidels sent his head in a silver box as a gift to the caliph of Baghdad."

"The same battle in which we lost Edessa and much of Antioch," Simon commented grimly.

"The very same." She slanted him a quick glance. "Baldwin has sworn to recover all the lost territories. As have the patriarch of Jerusalem and the grand masters of both the Templars and the Hospitallers. You will see much fighting in the months to come."

It was his turn to shrug. "Fighting is what I know."

And all he was likely to know, she acknowledged with a tightness in her chest. Except, of course, the honor and glory of serving God. He would have no wife. No sons to carry on his name. No daughters to comfort him when he grew too old to swing a sword.

Longing swift and sharp pierced Jocelyn's breast. How she ached to wed a knight like Simon de Rhys!

One who would give her sons and daughters strong and steady of purpose. A knight honorable to a fault, she added on a smothered sigh.

She could not but wonder at the twists of fate that had bound him to a dissolute father's vow and her to a king who would deliver her like a sack of gold besants to a would-be ally.

The irony of their respective positions dogged her thoughts for the rest of that day and into the night. It was still with her when her cavalcade topped a rise and the walls of Jerusalem appeared in the distance.

The sight of those golden-hued walls both humbled Simon and filled him with awe. This city was the goal of every pilgrim, every Crusader. It was why they left all that was familiar, why they traveled so many thousands of leagues and endured such hardships. And why he would spend the rest of his life with sword in hand, defending the holy sites within its encircling walls.

He could see the massive round dome of the mosque that the Crusaders had rechristened the Temple of Moriah when they retook the city during the First Crusade. Within a stone's throw of that, he knew, was the Western Wall. It was all that remained of Solomon's second temple, destroyed by the Romans along with the rest of Jerusalem some seventy years after the death of Christ.

And adjacent to the wall, he thought with a quickening of his pulse, was the building that housed the headquarters of the Poor Fellow-Soldiers of Christ and the Temple of Solomon. He knew well the rumors that swirled about the order's chosen site. Some said the first Grand Master had petitioned for just that location. Others suggested the Templars had tunneled through the wall in search of the Ark of the Covenant reputedly hidden from the Romans so many centuries ago. Still others whispered that they'd found the sacred relic and secreted it away in one of their great fortresses so it might be kept safe.

Simon had no idea as to the truth of any of these rumors, but the fact that he, too, would soon join this world-renowned order of warrior monks flooded him with both awe and a secret dismay.

He speared a glance at the woman beside him. Until she'd burst into his life, he'd resigned himself to becoming a Knight Templar. With some regrets, to be sure, but none that he could not live with. Now he would have to work doubly hard to empty his mind of the raw, carnal desire just the memory of her would rouse in him. His jaw tight, he turned his attention back to the great dome.

Using it as a beacon, he jostled for space so their entourage might take the road that led to the fabled Lion's Gate. The way was so crowded with pilgrims and merchants and knights and mendicant monks begging alms for the poor that when the gates burst open and a heavily armed troop emerged, the throngs of wayfarers had to leap out of the way.

Simon had no difficulty recognizing the royal standard fluttering at the head of the column. It displayed the same large cross and four smaller crosses as the seal on the missive Jocelyn had received.

"That's the king's standard," he said with a sudden tightening in his chest.

"I see it," she replied tersely.

Two standards flanked the king's pennant. The one on the left showed a gilded swan on a field of blue. Jocelyn identified it for him with a low exclamation.

"That's Queen Melisande's standard. She rides with her son."

The banner fluttering on the other side of the king's was the Beauseant of the Knights Templar. Beau for "noble" or "grand." Seant translated "to be." Both a symbol and a cry to battle, the banner's simple design of a plain white field above an equally plain field of black was recognized by friends and feared by foes throughout the known world. As long as the Beauseant flew, no Templar would quit the battlefield. And as long as a single Templar stood bloody but unconquered, the Beauseant would fly.

That flag represented Simon's destiny. Everything he would relinquish in the secular world. Everything he would gain in the spiritual. Never before had he felt so torn between those two realms.

When the thundering cavalcade approached their small entourage, he spotted a heavily armored knight in the lead. A gold coronet decorated his helm. It sparkled in the afternoon light when the man drew rein mere yards away. With a jangle of arms and shields, the rest of the troop followed his lead.

"Lady Jocelyn!"

She bowed her head. "My liege."

So this was Baldwin, the son and grandson of kings. Simon formed a swift impression of a bold, handsome face and shoulder-length gold-red hair showing beneath the helm. He should have hacked it off, Simon thought dispassionately. That hair would mark him as a target as surely as the gold coronet.

The woman beside the king possessed older but no less striking features. Despite the lines at the corners of her eyes, Queen Melisande exuded the vitality of a woman half her years. But it was the man on Baldwin's right who riveted Simon's attention.

Bernard de Tremelay, Grand Master of the Knights Templar. Thin to the point of desiccation, de Tremelay wore a square helm, a coat and hood of finely polished mail and the Templar's white surcoat emblazoned with a red cross. His eyes seemed to burn everything they touched. Simon felt their searing heat before the king's terse question reclaimed his attention.

"Why are you here, lady? Did I not send word

that you were to ready yourself for a journey to Damascus?"

"You did, sir, but I've come to speak with you about that."

"You've made your feelings about marriage to the emir clear enough," the king snapped. "I have neither the time nor the desire to discuss it with you yet again."

The whip in his voice drew Jocelyn's brows together, but she forebore to press the issue. Instead, her gaze swept the heavily armed troop.

"May I ask why you're so pressed, sir? What has occurred?"

"The Fatamids have taken Blanche Garde."

"By all the—!" she gasped. "Blanche Garde is one of the strongest keeps in the kingdom. How could it fall?"

"We're told it was by treachery within," the king answered grimly. "We go now to retake it."

Jocelyn didn't so much as hesitate. "I'll go as well."

"No, lady. We must needs ride hard and fast. You will remain here in Jerusalem."

The tempered steel Simon had glimpsed when she'd urged her mount onto a rickety wooden bridge surfaced once again. She glanced from the king to his mother and back again. She didn't state outright that she could ride as hard and fast as Queen Melisande, but the implication was clear to all. Then the Lady of Fortemur showed her colors.

"One scribbled line from me will put twenty mounted knights, a company of archers and a full complement of foot soldiers to arms. If my men know I ride with you, my liege, they will not eat or sleep until they reach my side."

The truth of her words weren't lost on either the king or his mother. Vassals owed their overlord only a specified number of men-at-arms, and then only for an agreed-upon number of days each year. Such arrangements made fielding an army on short notice difficult at best. Baldwin was not such a fool as to dismiss this chance to augment his hurriedly assembled forces.

"Then you will ride with me, lady." His glance shifted to Simon. "Is this one of your knights? I recognize him not."

"Allow me to present Simon de Rhys, Your Majesty. He's newly come to Outremer."

"De Rhys?"

Simon stiffened as the king's shrewd eyes measured him up and down. To his relief, it appeared the rumors concerning Gervase de Rhys had not yet reached his ear.

"Have you sworn allegiance to Lady Jocelyn, de Rhys? Or do you hope to serve the Crown?"

"I would serve her or you gladly, sir."

None but Jocelyn knew what it cost him to continue. He couldn't look at her as he did.

"But I am pledged to the Knights of the Temple."

The Grand Master leaned around the king to give Simon a sharp glance. "You are an aspirant to our order?"

"I am, Your Grace."

"Why did you not join before you took ship for Outremer?"

"There was not time to undergo the initiation."

"Nor is there time now," the king said, impatient to be on his way. "You may attend to the matter once we retake Blanche Garde, de Rhys. Betimes, Lady Jocelyn has seen fit to make you captain of her guard. You will continue in that capacity until relieved of your charge."

"Yes, sir."

"And you, Lady Jocelyn, will attach yourself to my lady mother's train. Now, for the sake of my kingdom and the God we all serve, let us away!"

Jocelyn took only enough time to pen a hurried note to Sir Hugh and pluck the few things from her traveling trunk that she deemed necessary. She sent Lady Beatrix back to Fortemur with the note, the two pages and sufficient guard to see them safe. The queen's entourage included more than enough women and pages to see to her needs.

Then she and Simon and the remainder of her troop fell into place for what they knew would be a grueling ride.

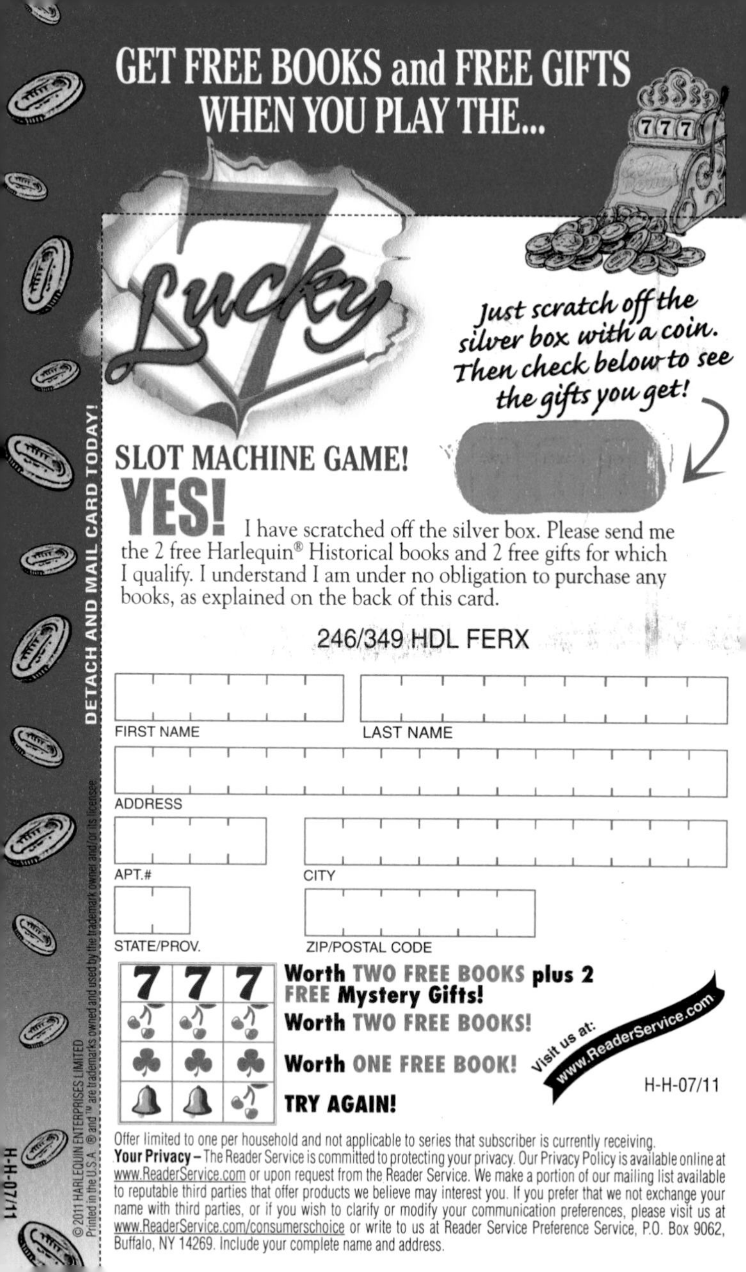
GET FREE BOOKS and FREE GIFTS
WHEN YOU PLAY THE...
777
Lucky 7
Just scratch off the silver box with a coin. Then check below to see the gifts you get!
SLOT MACHINE GAME!
YES! I have scratched off the silver box. Please send me the 2 free Harlequin® Historical books and 2 free gifts for which I qualify. I understand I am under no obligation to purchase any books, as explained on the back of this card.
246/349 HDL FERX
FIRST NAME
LAST NAME
ADDRESS
APT.#
CITY
STATE/PROV.
ZIP/POSTAL CODE
Worth TWO FREE BOOKS plus 2 FREE Mystery Gifts!
Worth TWO FREE BOOKS!
Worth ONE FREE BOOK!
TRY AGAIN!
Visit us at: www.ReaderService.com
H-H-07/11
Offer limited to one per household and not applicable to series that subscriber is currently receiving.
Your Privacy – The Reader Service is committed to protecting your privacy. Our Privacy Policy is available online at www.ReaderService.com or upon request from the Reader Service. We make a portion of our mailing list available to reputable third parties that offer products we believe may interest you. If you prefer that we not exchange your name with third parties, or if you wish to clarify or modify your communication preferences, please visit us at www.ReaderService.com/consumerschoice or write to us at Reader Service Preference Service, P.O. Box 9062, Buffalo, NY 14269. Include your complete name and address.
DETACH AND MAIL CARD TODAY!
© 2011 HARLEQUIN ENTERPRISES LIMITED
Printed in the U.S.A. ® and ™ are trademarks owned and used by the trademark owner and/or its licensee
H-H-07/11

Chapter Nine

Blanche Garde. The White Guard.

The name suited it, Simon decided when he drew rein on a distant rise and surveyed the fortress crowning a high, chalky outcropping. He was drenched in sweat and caked with grime from a journey that had covered more than twenty leagues in just over twenty-four hours. Yet he needed little more than a glance to appreciate the truth of King Baldwin's assessment. The castle could only have been taken by treachery. Its walls were too strong, its hilltop position too commanding.

"By the bones of St. John!"

The smothered exclamation came from young Will Farrier. For all his lack of experience ahorse, the lad had managed to keep up during the ride. He would ache clear to his soul when at last they made camp, though.

"Are those...?" He swiped his tongue over dust-caked lips and gaped at the plumes of black smoke rising from within Blanche Garde's massive curtain wall. "Are those funeral pyres?"

Simon dipped his chin in a curt nod. He'd seen his share and more of such pyres. They were lit to burn the corpses of those who'd fallen in battle or been put to the sword afterward. The dead must needs be disposed of quickly in heat such as this to prevent pestilence or disease. From the number of black plumes, it appeared that few of Blanche Garde's defenders had survived the surprise attack.

He dragged his gaze from the curling smoke to the army he'd ridden with. It was separating into two columns to take up positions surrounding the chalky prominence Blanche Garde occupied. The king's forces were as yet too few to launch a full-scale assault. Until more of his barons arrived to augment the ranks and his engineers had constructed the necessary siege engines and scaling towers, all Baldwin could do was contain the enemy within Blanche Garde's walls and attempt to negotiate a surrender.

There was little chance of that, Simon guessed. The very fact that the Fatamids had resorted to trickery to take the castle suggested it must have been well supplied to withstand a long siege. Those same supplies would now fortify Blanche Garde's occupiers for months, if not years.

His thoughts filling with strategies and tactics

employed during a siege, Simon signaled to Fortemur's contingent to follow him. Moments later he staked claim to a campsite close to a copse of almond trees. The thick-trunked trees would provide shade as well as defense. More to the point, they were fed by a tickling, rock-strewn spring that would slake the raging thirst of both man and beast.

Once he'd set them to constructing temporary shelters and had put Will to work currying the tired horses, he shed his helmet, pushed back his mailed hood and went to see how Jocelyn fared.

He found her without much difficulty. The king's men had pitched Baldwin's red-and-yellow-striped tent on a rise that gave a clear view of the hilltop fortress. His mother's blue tent was lavishly embroidered with gilded swans and sat farther back behind the lines. The Templars, Simon saw, had taken up a position opposite the castle's main sally port so they might be the first line of defense against any attack launched by those who now held Blanche Garde.

Although the king had set such a pace that it would be at least another day, maybe two, before the supply wagons caught up, his keen-eyed archers had brought down doe, wild boar, quail and rabbits en route. The king's marshal had also requisitioned olives, fruits, ale and grain from the farms and villages they'd passed through. As a consequence, meat already sizzled on spits and a small army of pages and squires hurried about the camp seeing to their masters' needs. Simon stopped one wearing the queen's colors outside the blue-flocked tent.

"You, lad. Inquire within of the Lady Jocelyn of Fortemur. Tell her Simon de Rhys would speak with her."

The page ducked inside the tent. He ducked out again some moments later and held the flap up for Jocelyn to emerge.

Simon could not believe the hunger that reared up and clawed at him like a sharp-taloned beast. He had but to look at her to feel his heart jerk and his breath slide back down his throat.

She'd washed off her travel grime and tamed her hair by parting it in the center and catching the sides back. She still wore her traveling gown but had shed her cloak. In the early-evening light her lips had the hue of a ripe peach. The need to taste them put a brusque edge to his words.

"Are you well disposed, lady?"

"Well enough." She gave the tent behind her a rueful glance. "Melisande has ridden the length and breadth of this kingdom a dozen times or more during her years as both queen and regent. She's a seasoned campaigner. You need not fear for my comfort or safety."

Simon had to admit the times bred remarkable women. Like Eleanor of Aquitaine, Melisande of Jerusalem had more than proved herself. Daughter to one king, mother to another, she'd governed a kingdom beset by enemies on all sides for more than two decades.

Jocelyn of Fortemur was bred of the same stock. So Simon wasn't surprised that she was more concerned about her people's comfort than her own.

"What of my men? Where are they positioned?"

He gestured toward the stand of almond trees fed by the rocky creek. "They're there, just beyond that copse."

"Show me."

They wove their way past hastily erected tents and shelters to the trees. Their leaves were a rubbery green, their trunks were as thick around as a baker's midsection. Simon took Jocelyn's arm to help her navigate the uneven ground, then stood quietly while she conferred with the sergeant of her guard.

"Sir Simon made sure we are well provisioned," the burly lancer assured her. "We have ale and meats and feed for the horses and mules."

She turned to the youth hauling a bucket of water from the stream. "And you, Will? How do you fare in your new duties as squire?"

The farrier's son made a gallant attempt at a smile. "I ache from my head to my toes, lady. Just as Sir Simon promised I would."

"You'll ache more before this is done, I fear."

"So I am told."

Jocelyn didn't miss the lad's quick, deferential glance at his new master. She could see it had taken de Rhys only a few days to earn his respect and that of her small troop.

Even less to earn hers.

She couldn't help but think of how it had taken him mere hours to change from the filthy, ragtag slave she'd purchased in El-Arish to the steel-voiced knight who'd ordered her to remove both her clothing and his. To this day Jocelyn wasn't sure how he'd turned the tables on her so swiftly.

Now he was back in his own milieu. He ordered the disposition of her men with the instinctive air of one used to command. They sensed that he knew whereof he spoke and followed without hesitation where he led.

Confident that she could leave them in his care, she addressed the sergeant of her guard once more. "Sir Hugh should arrive late this night or early in the morning with supplies and reinforcements."

"Aye, lady. Sir Simon told us."

"Until the morrow, then."

"Until the morrow. God keep you."

Simon fell in beside her as they retraced their steps. Smiling, she commented on her observation that he'd won the trust of her men.

"Your name falls readily from their lips."

"Not nearly as often as yours does." He held a branch aside for her. "They do you credit, lady. They're well trained and quick to follow orders."

"That's more Sir Hugh's doing than mine."

"I beg to differ. Everyone in a keep, from the boys who muck the stables to the most senior knight, take their tone from their lord. Or in this case, their lady."

She acknowledged the truth of his comment with a shrug that in no way made light of the burden she carried night and day. She'd been born to high honors. They were her right, and her constant, unceasing responsibility.

Her steps slowed and she paused in a patch of shade. In truth she was in no great hurry to return to the queen's tent. It was a noisy, crowded place. The nobles who'd supported Melisande in her struggle to hold on to the reins of power still deferred to her judgment. Her son's adherents were no less loath to seek the advice of one who'd ruled so wisely for so many years. Even Baldwin had made an appearance at his mother's tent soon after they'd encamped, with promises to return again to share the evening meal.

When he did, Jocelyn would ask to speak privately with him. She hadn't forgotten the reason for her hasty journey. How could she? With this latest incursion by the Fatamids, an alliance with the Emir of Damascus had become even more crucial. Her chest went tight at the thought of the firestorm that would erupt when she revealed her altered state and—she prayed!—unsuitability as a bride for Ali ben Haydar.

Swallowing her fears, she ran a palm over the scaly

bark of a low-hanging branch and lifted her gaze to Simon's. He'd removed his helmet and pushed back his mail hood, leaving his hair to stand in sweaty spikes. She had to dig her nails into the bark to keep from reaching up to smooth the strands.

"Will you remove to the Templars' camp when Sir Hugh arrives?"

He didn't pretend to misunderstand her. They both knew they'd been gifted by these few extra days together. They dared not tempt fate by demanding more.

"I think it best."

"Do you…? Do you wish me to ask the king if he'll stand sponsor to you with the Grand Master? It would speed your initiation."

The blue eyes looking down into her darkened. "I can't ask more of you than you've already given me."

How she ached for this man's touch. Longed for his kiss. Was she so perverse that she wanted only what she could not have?

"I could give you more, Simon." The words spilled out before she could stop them. "I could beg the king for a different boon. Ask him to speak with the Grand Master about releasing you from your father's vow."

She saw hope flare in his eyes, swiftly come and just as swiftly gone.

"I won't forswear myself."

His insistence on clinging to the shreds of his father's honor stirred a welter of most contradictory emotions in Jocelyn's breast. Admiration and frustration. Pride and despair. Atop all swirled the realization that by holding fast to his vow he would be lost to her forever.

She'd been raised by a grandsire who would cut off his arm before he would lift a sword against his sworn liege. Three days ago she would have wagered all she owned that her grandfather's blood ran true in her. Never had she dreamed that she would ask—or allow—a man to go back on an oath once given. Yet she couldn't hold in an urgent plea that he rethink his obligation.

"You're not responsible for your father's sins, Simon."

When he stood stubbornly silent, her frustration flared into reckless determination. She pressed her hips against the low-hanging branch, tipped her head and laid her palms on his broad chest.

"Nor should you allow him to bind you to a life of celibacy."

Still he wouldn't speak. Goaded, she dug her fingertips in the leather surcoat covering his mail.

"You've given me a taste of the pleasures a man and woman may share. Do you not wish to show me more? Do you not want me, as you've made me want you?"

Hundreds of armed men were camped within

shouting distance. Smoke from their cook fires and from the pyres of Blanche Garde drifted on the air. Yet the thick branches and screen of green, rubbery leaves gave her the illusion that there were only the two of them. Alone. Together. This one last time.

"Let me speak to the king," Jocelyn pleaded. "Or to the queen. If you prove yourself here, they would grant you a holding. You could take a wife. Have sons and daughters to give you comfort. Hell's teeth, Simon, don't you want someone who will love you and—"

With a snarl, he fisted his hands around her upper arms.

"Yes, I want that! And you, Jocelyn. I ache for you. So much I must needs use every ounce of my will to keep from spinning you around, bending you over that branch and dragging up your skirts so I might bury myself in your hot, wet flesh. Is that what you wish to hear?"

It was! Of a certainty, it was!

Her triumph must have shown in her eyes because the face so close to her own hardened. She read his intent even as he swooped down to cover her mouth with his.

The kiss was meant to punish, and it did. His lips ground against hers. His fingers dug into the flesh of her upper arms. She felt their bite before he loosed his hands and banded an arm around her waist. Widening his stance, he hauled her hard against his chest.

Too late Jocelyn realized she'd prodded a sleeping dragon. She couldn't escape its ferocious assault. Nor, she admitted as her blood pounded in her veins, did she wish to.

This wasn't the cold, dispassionate knight who'd ordered her to remove her robes. Nor yet the skilled lover who'd brought her to such exquisite pleasure. This was a man with his blood up. One who at the least sign of surrender would take her as violently as he'd threatened.

She came within a hairbreadth of that surrender. Every part of her ached to feel again the exquisite torment of his fingers stroking her flesh. His rigid shaft stretching her. His length filling her.

Yet even as she opened her mouth to the brutal assault of his tongue and teeth, she knew she couldn't destroy what she admired most in this man. Whether she willed it or not, he held his honor dearer than his life. And would come to hate her if she stripped it from him.

Gasping, she tried to pull away. He countered by shoving a hand through her hair to hold her head still. His mouth took hers.

"Simon!" Jocelyn broke her lips away as she pounded his unyielding form. "Simon, I beg you..."

It took some moments for her protests to pierce his unleashed lust. When they did, his head came up.

His eyes burned into hers for long moments before he thrust her away almost violently.

"Get you back to the queen's tent."

She couldn't leave him like this. In a futile effort to soothe the fearsome creature she'd released from its chains, she held out a hand.

"Simon…"

"Now, woman!"

Jocelyn could count on the fingers of one hand the number of times she'd cowered in the face of danger. This was one of them. Grasping her skirts in shaking hands, she fled the copse of almond trees.

Simon didn't call her back, although keeping silent took every shred of his iron will.

She wanted him. As much as he wanted her. She'd ripped the truth from the depths of his soul, and now he must live with the echo of that raw admission for the rest of his life. Every time he knelt in prayer, he would have to force his mind to God instead of thoughts of her. Every time he swung a sword in battle, his enemy would have the face of the man Jocelyn would soon wed.

The thought of another man's hands and mouth on her took everything that Simon was and twisted it in knots. Not for the first time since Jocelyn had taken him to her bed, he considered forswearing himself. According to the Bishop of Clairvaux, such an act would condemn his dissolute sire—and himself—to eternal damnation. Right now, with the taste of her still on his lips and his blood clamoring for more, Simon would count the cost well worth it.

Slowly, like the insistent rays of the sun burning through a gray mist, reason reasserted itself. Even if he did abandon his honor and all thoughts of joining the Knights Templar, Jocelyn was the Lady of Fortemur, with all the honors and chains that came with it. Neither the king nor his mother would consider giving such a rich prize to the landless younger son of a knight whose very name carried the stink of dishonor.

His face as bleak as his soul, Simon spit out a foul oath and turned toward the camp.

Jocelyn's chest didn't stop heaving or her knees shaking until she was in the shadow of the queen's tent. Even then she had to fold her arms around her waist and pace outside until her heart slowed its frantic hammering.

It had yet to resume a regular beat when a page scurried out of the tent and held up the flap. A moment later, Queen Melisande herself emerged. Her jeweled coronet sparkled in the waning light, as did the gold and silver stitchery in the surcoats of the two nobles who followed her out.

Jocelyn was too unsettled to join the queen. Succumbing to a cowardly urge, she tried to duck behind the tent. She'd taken only one quick step, however, before Melisande spotted her.

"Lady Jocelyn?"

She dipped into a curtsy. "Majesty."

"What have you been about?"

"I was seeing to the disposition of my men."

The queen's delicately arched brows drew into a straight line. Hooking an imperious finger, she commanded Jocelyn to approach.

"Why are your cheeks so flushed?"

"Are they flushed?" Shrugging, she tried to feign nonchalance. "I must have walked overfast."

The face stamped on so many of the coins minted in the Kingdom of Jerusalem over the years took on a hard cast. Melisande didn't posses the straight, classical nose or willowy neck sung of by troubadours. But her red-gold hair showed only a few traces of silver and her grip was firm as she pinched Jocelyn's chin between thumb and forefinger and tipped her face to the light.

"Don't play me for a fool, girl." She cast a swift look at the pages, squires and courtiers observing their exchange with great interest and lowered her voice. "Do you think I don't recognize the scrape a man's whiskers leave on a woman's cheeks and chin?"

"My lady..."

"Speak me no lies. Where have you been?"

"To see to my men. I swear it."

"And which of those men put his mark on you?"

Dear sweet Lord! Jocelyn was fully prepared to accept the consequences of her desperate measures to avoid marriage to the emir. She'd known she would draw the king's ire down on her head. The queen's, as well, since Melisande concurred in the match.

But she would not have their wrath fall on Simon. Cursing the perversity that had made her tempt him to such violence that he'd left his mark on her, Jocelyn scrambled for an explanation that would satisfy the queen without endangering Simon. She could find none.

When she remained mute, Melisande's eyes narrowed. "By all the saints! Are you besotted with some lowly knave who—"

She broke off and sucked in a swift breath.

"The knight who rode with you. The one who says he's pledged to the Templars. I saw how he looked at you, and you at him. Is that who put this red in your cheeks and such despair in your heart?"

Fear for him drained whatever heat had been in Jocelyn's cheeks. Cold to her bones, she shook her head. "If you sense despair, Majesty, it's because of the marriage you and the king force on me."

The queen's mouth hardened. "You know how important this alliance is. So important that the king sent an urgent missive to the emir requesting he meet us here and claim his bride."

"What?"

"Ali ben Haydar marches even now to join his army with ours."

Feeling as though the ground had just shifted under her feet, Jocelyn made a desperate appeal. "Please hear me on this, milady. I cannot go willingly into marriage with him."

"I understand your reluctance," the queen said in what she obviously intended as a soothing tone. "Truly, I do. But too much rides on this union for us to give way to the tears and vapors of a frightened virgin."

Jocelyn swallowed, dragged in a deep breath and lifted her chin. When her eyes met those of the queen, she didn't speak. She didn't have to. Melisande guessed the truth almost immediately.

"Oh, you foolish, foolish girl," she hissed. "What have you done?"

"I—"

"Not here! Come inside. We must needs speak privately about this."

Her heart stuttering, Jocelyn followed Melisande into her luxuriously appointed tent. As she'd assured Simon, the royal matriarch was well used to traveling the length and breadth of the kingdom. That in no way prevented her from bringing with her all she required for her comfort.

Persian carpets in rich jewel tones covered the ground. Hammered-brass lamps hung on chains from the tent poles. Folding chairs were arranged around strapped campaign trunks that doubled as eating and writing tables.

The queen's scribe sat at one of the trunks, scribbling furiously with a quill. Her chief lady-in-waiting directed a page on the proper way to set out gold plates and goblets on another trunk. Melisande wasted no time in dismissing all three.

"Leave us, Lady Sybil. Take the others with you."

Her tone invited no question or hesitation. Lady, scribe and page hurried to obey. When the flap dropped behind them, Melisande herself splashed wine into two goblets. She thrust one into Jocelyn's hand and drank from the other before giving the younger woman a look that sliced like a claymore.

"I've known you since you were in swaddling clothes. Your mother served me well in the first years of her marriage. Your grandsire fought at my father's side. So do not think to fob me off with lies or half truths."

Pinned by her unrelenting stare, Jocelyn could only nod.

"Now, tell me what in the name of all the saints you've done."

Chapter Ten

The moment Jocelyn had schemed for and dreaded in equal parts had arrived. Yet now that she'd come to the point of revealing what she'd done, she was caught in a trap of her own making.

Why in God's name had she taunted Simon into such rough kisses? His beard had all but branded her. Now she would have to dance over dangerously hot coals to shield him from the queen's wrath.

"I wrote to you and to the king both regarding my feelings toward marriage to the emir," she began.

"Yes, you did. Several times." Melisande waved an impatient hand. "If ben Haydar had desired any other holdings but yours, we would have offered him a different bride. But Fortemur will give him the access to the sea he's long desired. And you, Jocelyn, are Fortemur."

"I won't be if I wed the emir," she retorted with

more heat than wisdom. "I'll become but one of his many wives, shut away in a harem. I will not live such a life, milady."

"Will not?" The queen's head snapped up. "You forget yourself, girl! You are a royal ward. You will wed who we say."

"I do not forget. How could I?"

She struggled to keep bitterness from coloring her voice. Melisande had put the needs of her kingdom ahead of her own since the day of her birth. Somehow, someway, Jocelyn must convince her that those needs could be met by other means than this loathsome marriage.

"I could grant the emir's caravans right of passage through my lands. Mayhap a portion of the port taxes. Surely that would satisfy his demands."

"Grants may be revoked. Wives may not. In most cases," the queen was forced to add.

"The emir doesn't want a wife." Jocelyn couldn't control the bitterness now. It came from deep inside and spilled into her voice. "He wants an untried virgin to take to his bed. One he may bloody his shaft on. It's said he gets no pleasure unless he causes pain."

"Where did you hear such salacious rumors?"

"Where did I not! It's common knowledge, Majesty."

"It's gossip of the most mean sort."

Her tone was so cold and unyielding that Jocelyn

knew she had to take another tack. In a last, desperate attempt, she appealed to the queen's piety.

"As you reminded me not moments ago, you've known me since I was in swaddling clothes. Like you, I was taught from my earliest days to manage my holdings. Now you would have me relinquish that authority and give my birthright to a nonbeliever."

"A nonbeliever who tolerates all faiths."

Jocelyn's heart sank. Piety, obviously, ran together with politics in the mind of a woman who'd given every day of her life to maintaining Christian control of the Holy Land.

"Need I remind you that this union has the blessing of the Church?" the queen continued coldly. "The Patriarch of Jerusalem himself reviewed the marriage contracts and is satisfied that you'll be allowed to practice your own religion."

"And will the Patriarch convince my lord and husband to let me confess my sins to a priest? I'm told the only males his wives may have discourse with are eunuchs."

She realized her mistake the moment the words passed her lips. Melisande seized on them immediately.

"So it's discourse you want, is it?" Her shrewd eyes raked Jocelyn's cheek and chin. "Is that what you did with the knight pledged to the Templars? The one I suspect left those marks on your face?"

"Majesty..."

"Surely you know once your knight takes his vows he cannot contact you again, much less have discourse."

Jocelyn could not falter now. Simon's life hung in the balance. Shrugging, she tried to deflect the arrow aimed at him.

"The king himself requested de Rhys continue as captain of my guard. Until then, he must needs speak with me."

"Speak with?" the queen echoed slowly, dangerously. "Or give you the means to escape this marriage you so despise. Have you laid with him?"

"No!"

Her response was too swift, too forceful, and spoke more of desperation than indignation. Melisande saw through it immediately.

"Tell me, girl. Are you maid or not?"

"I..."

"Tell me," the queen ordered, her eyes blazing, "else I will summon my physician and have him examine you before a tentful of witnesses."

"No, I am not a maid."

Throwing aside her goblet, Melisande lashed out with an openhanded slap that sent Jocelyn staggering backward.

"You fool! You headstrong, selfish fool. You know how much we need the army that the emir brings with him. You've not only put our kingdom at risk, you've put de Rhys's head on the block."

"It wasn't him! I swear by all that is holy."

Until that moment Jocelyn didn't know—couldn't know—how deeply she held Simon in her heart. Before, her only concerns were to spare herself a loathsome marriage and him the king's wrath. Now she would consign her very soul to the devil to keep him safe.

"I gave myself to Geoffrey," she said desperately.

"Geoffrey?"

"Geoffrey de Lusignan. You must remember him. My grandsire arranged for us to wed after the first lord I was betrothed to fell in battle."

The queen's brows snapped together. "Aye, I remember de Lusignan."

"He was young." Near tripping over her tongue, Jocelyn wove a hurried web of truths and lies. "Young and merry. And so handsome his mere kiss threw me into girlish raptures. I…I laid with him before he rode into battle for the last time."

"You were but a child then! You couldn't have celebrated more than ten name days."

"Eleven. I'd celebrated my eleventh name day. Although my grandsire decreed me still too young to consummate the marriage, I'd started my courses. I was a woman in the eyes of God and the law. You yourself were only a year older when you wed the Count of Anjou."

The pointed reminder of the queen's turbulent marriage made Melisande stiffen.

"The difference," she said frigidly, "is that I did my duty and wed where my father said I must. As will you, Jocelyn, if the emir will still have you."

"Majesty, I implore you..."

No!" She flung up a hand. "Don't say another word. I cannot allow you to jeopardize everything I've worked for these many years. We need this alliance most desperately to protect our western borders. So, too, do we need the army the emir brings to help us retake Blanche Garde."

Jocelyn could see in her face that the happiness of one royal ward was a small price to pay for the safety of an entire kingdom. Melisande and her son would throw her to the wolves to seal this fragile alliance. She could only hope that the emir would repudiate the proposed marriage once he learned she was no maid.

If he learned.

With a sickening feeling in the pit of her stomach, she realized neither the king nor his mother was beyond sending her to the emir despite her altered state. God alone knew what might happen if Ali ben Haydar took her to bed and discovered he'd been duped.

As if echoing her thoughts, Melisande pointed to the tent flap. "Get you gone. I must think how best to deal with this turn of events."

"Please, Majesty..."

"Go."

Sick at heart, Jocelyn got to her feet. The deepening purple haze that greeted her when she emerged made her blink in confusion. Her mind was in such turmoil that she'd lost all sense of time.

Was it just a short while since Simon had responded to her taunt? A half a turn of the hourglass since she'd felt his mouth on hers? It might have happened in another lifetime.

Desolation filled her as she looked around the bustling camp with unseeing eyes. She felt lost. Defeated. And alone. So very alone.

The waves of self-pity that washed through her were as uncharacteristic as they were unwelcome. Then she remembered that she wasn't the only one caught in this damnable coil.

Had the queen believed the lies she'd spouted? Was Simon safe, or would Melisande call him to account for the marks he'd made on her?

If she did, Jocelyn knew with sickening certainty, Simon would speak the truth. His honor wouldn't allow him to do otherwise. Oh, he wouldn't reveal what had happened the night she'd brought him back from El-Arish. He'd sworn never to speak of that and he wouldn't. His honor wouldn't allow it.

But he'd sworn no such oath about their time together in the crystal cave. She hadn't thought to ask it of him. If pressed, he might speak the truth about that to save her from a marriage he knew she despised.

And he would die for it.

Terror closed her throat. She had to warn him. Convince him somehow, someway, to deny that they'd coupled. Or at least remain mute. He could do that, she thought as her fear for him clogged her lungs. He could say nothing at all and, by his silence, acquiesce in her lie.

Lifting her skirts, she began to run, and startled faces turned when she passed. Gruff voices called out to her.

"Milady!"

"What's amiss?"

She didn't get far. Less than twenty paces from the queen's tent a familiar figure appeared in the deepening dusk.

"Hugh!" Near sobbing with relief at the sight of her most trusted confidant and adviser, she flung herself at his chest. "When did you arrive?"

"Just now. I brought Sir Guy, and the full complement of knights and men-at-arms that you ordered. De Rhys told me I would find you here, so I came straightaway in search of you."

When she continued to cling to him, he patted her back awkwardly.

"What's amiss, lady? Why do you weep?"

"I...I confessed to the queen."

"The saints preserve us! You told her everything?"

"Yes. No." She fought down the fear that threatened

to choke her and shoved away from the comfort of his arms. "I let her know I'm no longer a maid, but I said it was Geoffrey de Lusignan I laid with."

"De Lusignan!" Sir Hugh's brows soared above his weathered face. "You were scarce out of short skirts when he fell in battle. The queen could not have believed he bedded you."

"She did. She must." She gripped his arms and dug her fingers into his mail. "You must tell Simon, Hugh. Now, before she questions him."

Astonishment at her bold-faced lie gave way to confusion. The castellan shook his head and tried to make sense of her breathless disclosures.

"I don't understand. If you told Melisande you laid with Geoffrey de Lusignan, why would she question de Rhys?"

"I met with him earlier." Her hands went to her cheeks. "His...his beard scraped my face. The queen saw the marks and guessed their source."

"Saints preserve us, Jocelyn!"

"I know," she said miserably. "I've twisted matters beyond measure. Just tell Simon what I have done, Hugh, before the queen summons him to her tent. Convince him to put aside his thrice-damned honor and go along with my lie."

He gave her a look she'd never before seen on his face. Was it disapproval? Disappointment? A combination of both, she realized as he shook his head again.

"Never did I think to hear the Lady of Fortemur scorn a man for holding to his honor."

"It could well put his head on the block!"

Breathing hard and fast, she fought the almost overwhelming feeling of despair over the morass she'd plunged both herself and Simon into.

"The queen repeated yet again how much she and the king desire an alliance with the emir. If the alliance falls through… If Simon shares the blame with me, he'll feel the full weight of their displeasure."

"You knew that before you drew him into your web of deceit."

"I thought I could preserve his identity! I thought he would be well gone from my life before I revealed my altered state to the king and his mother. Nor," she added, sick at heart, "did I imagine that my scheme would put at risk his intent to join the Knights Templar."

Bernard de Tremelay might field an army of knights who owed allegiance to none but him and the Pope, but the Templars' very existence was tied to the survival of Baldwin's kingdom. The Grand Master would back the king and his mother in whatever fate they decided for Simon.

"It's a fine coil you've landed de Rhys in, Jocelyn."

"I know," she said again, hanging her head.

The weight of Hugh's disapproval was crushing.

Her fear for Simon outweighed it by a thousand measures.

"Please, speak with him."

"And say what?"

"Tell him I cannot have him on my conscience. Tell him he must not admit we laid together or..."

Or what? What could induce Simon to lie, or at least keep silent?

"Or I will say he seeks only to protect me. That, in truth, I made up the whole tale of surrendering my maidenhead to escape a marriage the queen knows I despise."

"That's easily enough disproved."

"Mayhap. Mayhap not."

The bitter thoughts that had followed her out of the queen's tent came back with brutal force.

"As anxious as Melisande is to see this alliance done, she could well instruct the king's physician to confirm my virgin's shield is still intact. She could even have one of her ladies show me how to weep and writhe in pain and cut myself so that I bleed profusely when the emir takes me to bed."

"Jocelyn!"

"What? Don't say it can't be done. Shall I tell you which of my ladies used pig's blood to stain the sheets on her wedding night?"

That silenced him.

"Go to Simon, Hugh. Please! Tell him I will not have him bear the consequences of my rash acts."

The aged knight's face was little more than a blur in the deepening dusk, but Jocelyn saw his jaw work from side to side.

How had she brought him and Simon and herself to such a coil? When had matters become so tangled that not even an argonaut's sword could slice through the knots?

Shamed to her very soul, she stretched out a hand. The sudden ball of fire that launched into the sky behind him made her jerk it back.

"What…?"

The ball soared high in the purple sky, trailing a tail of brilliant sparks. Jocelyn recognized it for what it was immediately.

"Hugh!" she gasped. "Look!"

The knight spun around and spit out a violent oath. Like her, he needed only a glance to grasp what that blazing ball portended.

"Greek fire," he snarled through bared teeth.

The mere name was enough to inspire terror. First used by the Byzantines to repel Saracen attacks against Constantinople, the fiery projectiles had since become a staple of both besieging and besieged armies. Soldiers sprayed by the combination of flaming resin, quicklime and sulphur died most agonizing deaths. Wooden siege engines and towers burned to cinders.

But no siege engines had as yet been built. No wooden towers were ready to roll into position. And these balls of flame didn't come from the direction of Blanche Garde. Nor, Jocelyn realized in a moment of sheer panic, from the king's encamped army.

Another blazed into the sky. Then another, and another. In the next heartbeat, they crashed to earth right in the center of the camp. Screams rent the night. A tent became a flaming pyre.

They were being attacked from the rear! By the very army that was supposed to join forces with Baldwin's!

The realization burst on Jocelyn with the same searing impact as the projectiles now raining down on the camp. She had time for just that one, terrible thought before Hugh lunged forward and grasped her wrist.

Pivoting violently on one heel, he swung her like a weighted stone at the end of a tether. Shrieking, Jocelyn flew through the air. She hit with a force that knocked the air from her lungs. At the same instant, a fiery ball crashed to earth just paces from where she'd stood.

Where her castellan still stood.

"Noooooo!"

The scream ripped from her throat as tongues of fire spewed in all directions and turned everything they touched into a torch.

"Hugh!"

Panting, sobbing, propelled by sheer panic, she got her feet under her and thrust upward. By then her most trusted friend and adviser was ablaze. Fire licked at his boots, his surcoat, even his hair.

Chaos reigned and screams now filled the night. Ignoring all agonized cries but Sir Hugh's, Jocelyn looked frantically for a cloak or blanket. When she saw nothing close at hand, she dragged up the hem of her bliaut. Water wouldn't douse the fire, but maybe she could smother it with her robe.

She tried. She tried most desperately. Throwing herself to her knees, she slapped at Hugh's writhing form with the folds of her gown. Heat singed her face. The stench of burning flesh seared her nostrils.

She couldn't beat down the flames. They ate right through her bliaut and blistered her hands. In desperation, she screamed for help.

"Someone! Anyone! I beg of you, attend to me!"

Her frantic cries went unheeded. And no wonder. The scene that met her frantic eyes could have come from the lowest reaches of hell.

The unexpected attack had thrown the king's camp into mindless panic. Foot soldiers ran in every direction. Pages cowered in terror. Knights screamed at squires to fetch swords and shields and horses. All the while death rained down around them.

She was still on her knees, her breath rasping raw in her throat and her heart near stuttering with fear, when she heard her name shouted above the tumult.

"Jocelyn!"

She raised smoke-seared eyes and saw Simon charging through the flames. He'd drawn his sword. Donned his helm. Taken up his shield. Unlike so many others in the king's camp, he was prepared to battle whatever foe might appear through the carnage.

Jocelyn near wept with relief. He would save Sir Hugh. He must!

Yet she knew from the moment he halted beside her that he couldn't work miracles. She couldn't miss the grim assessment in his eyes as they skimmed over Hugh's charred flesh. That one glance said her desperate efforts had gone for naught.

"He's beyond help."

"No!"

"He's dead, Jocelyn, and you must get to shelter."

"I can't leave him. Simon! Hear me! I can't leave him."

He didn't waste time on debate. Reaching down, he pulled her to her feet and dragged her away from the smoking body. She fought him every step of the way, but she might have been a butterfly beating its wings against a steel cage. Ignoring her frantic protests, he raised his shield above his head to protect them both as best he could from flying tongues of fire.

In the midst of her fury and fear she heard a

drawn-out hiss above her. It was a low warning—their only warning—before the fires of hell consumed them both.

Chapter Eleven

The blazing ball tore off the top of the queen's tent. Spewing fire and death, it crashed to earth some yards beyond. The tent's blue cloth walls shook violently and collapsed in on themselves. Flames were already consuming the gilded swans when Jocelyn beat on Simon's arm and screamed to be heard over the uproar.

"The queen! Simon! The queen's inside her tent!"

He didn't hesitate. Throwing her to the ground in a tangle of arms and legs, he covered her with his shield.

"Stay here!"

Like a turtle in its shell, Jocelyn wiggled around frantically on her belly until she faced the now-flaming tent. Terror consumed her while she watched

Simon swing his sword two-handed to hack through fallen poles and burning cloth.

He would burn. His surcoat would flame. His face and hands would scorch. His chain mail would heat, and he would roast alive. She couldn't bear to crouch and tremble like a blancmange while he fought his way into that inferno. Throwing off the heavy shield, she leaped to her feet and screamed with all the power of her heat- and smoke-seared lungs.

"To the queen! To the queen!"

Her frantic cry brought Melisande's terror-stricken lady-in-waiting running from the pile of equipment she'd crouched behind. Along the way Lady Sybil rallied several cowering, quaking pages.

Jocelyn's frantic cry also caught the ear of a knight about to throw himself aboard his hastily saddled destrier. His head jerked around and horror filled his face beneath his helm. He shouted something to his squire and raced toward the queen's tent. Two of the king's guard came running at the same time.

Then the king himself appeared! Baldwin was mounted on his warhorse and had a small troop of knights scrambling to follow him.

"My lady mother?" he shouted at Jocelyn.

"She's within!"

With a vicious oath, he kicked free of the stirrups and would have thrown himself from the saddle if a terrifying apparition hadn't stumbled from the burning tent.

It was a man, or so Jocelyn thought. Covered from head to foot by one of the thick Persian carpets that had graced the floor of the tent. Flames were already licking at the rug, making it appear as though he wore a cloak of fire.

The horror around her seemed to fade. The shouts and screams died. For what felt like an eternity she couldn't move, couldn't breathe. Not until the apparition tore off his heavy covering and she spotted Queen Melisande clinging to Simon's chest, did Jocelyn draw in a raw, rasping breath.

She wanted to drop to her knees and give a sobbing prayer of thanksgiving. But even as the king's guards rushed forward to relieve Simon of his burden and the queen assured her anxious son that she was unhurt, a chorus of hoarse shouts heralded a new danger.

Jocelyn spun around and followed outthrust arms and pointing fingers. Horrified, she saw that Blanche Garde's massive gates had been thrown open. While she watched in swamping waves of dismay, the portcullis went up and the drawbridge rattled down. She didn't need to see the distinctive armor of the Saracen cavalry that thundered onto the drawbridge to realize the king's army had been lured into a well-planned trap.

Baldwin recognized it as well. Rising in the stirrups, he shouted at the knights behind him. "LeBeau! Tell the trumpeters to sound 'To Arms.' Ibelin, you take the left flank. DeChatillion, the right. I'll lead the center. We'll attack those who fire at us from the rear first."

The knights pulled on the reins, spurred their mounts and thundered in opposite directions.

"You!"

The king's glance cut to Simon. He couldn't remember his name but recalled who he was pledged to.

"Get you to the Templars. Tell the Grand Master he must blunt the attack from Blanche Garde at all costs."

He sawed on the reins to hold his mount steady as another fireball soared overhead.

"And you..." This was directed to the knight who'd rushed over on foot. "Take my lady mother and these women..."

Where? No tent was safe from the missiles raining down on them, no place secure from attack.

"The stream just beyond that copse of trees," Simon shouted as he raced to Jocelyn and scooped up the shield she'd thrown aside. "They can crouch below its bank."

"To the stream," the king concurred grimly as he dug his spurs into his mount's sides. "I'll send a troop to safeguard them as soon as I may."

Simon paused only to thrust his shield at Jocelyn. "Keep this to protect your head and back."

"No! You'll need it."

"I'll find another."

He was already off and running. Her arms sagging with the weight of the embossed leather shield, Jocelyn watched him dodge fiery obstacles with the agility of a panther. He stopped only to seize the reins of a riderless palfrey plunging through the chaos and haul himself into the saddle. By the time the trumpets sounded a strident call to arms, he'd disappeared from her sight.

"Majesty." The smoke-blackened knight the king had entrusted his mother to croaked out a desperate plea. "The copse of trees. We must get you there."

He held his shield over Melisande's and Lady Sibyl's heads. Jocelyn grunted at the weight of Simon's but raised it high enough to join with his. Under this pitifully inadequate protection, they stumbled past blazing tents and smoldering corpses to the rocky stream cutting through the trees.

Once there, the beleaguered knight thrust both shields into the bank. The queen and her lady-in-waiting crouched under them. They were up to their ankles in trickling water and surrounded on all sides by the din of men rushing to answer the trumpet's call. Melisande shoved her charred veil from her eyes and beckoned urgently to Jocelyn.

"Here, girl. Take cover with us."

Jocelyn started to duck under the shield but halted after just a step. Sir Hugh was dead. Simon had been sent to fight alongside the Templars. Who remained to lead Fortemur's contingent?

"I must see to my men."

"No!" Melisande reached out and grabbed her wrist. "Do not leave this shelter."

Shaking off her hold, Jocelyn crouched and followed the low, winding bank. Her sodden skirts dragged the mud. Rocks bit through the soles of her boots. Smoke stung her eyes.

The site Simon had selected for her troop lay close. She was certain of it. Or as certain as she could be of anything in this terrifying nightmare. She was about to climb up on the bank to take her bearings when a knight wearing the black and red of Fortemur charged through the trees.

"Sir Guy!"

Thank the Lord! Her armorer had arrived with Sir Hugh! Sobbing with relief, Jocelyn scrambled up the bank.

"Sir Guy! Here!"

"Milady!" Sawing on his mount's reins, he drew it to a pawing halt. "Sir Simon sent us to stand with you and the queen until the king's men arrive. Now, for the love of the Holy Virgin, take cover."

Since he'd already dismounted and was dragging her back down the bank, Jocelyn had no choice but to obey. Then all she could do was try to block the screams and stench and wing prayer after prayer heavenward.

Keep him safe.

Dear God, please keep him safe.

Simon thrust right, then left, then right again. Sweat poured down his face, soaked his neck beneath his mail. His sword was blooded to the hilt. Its grip was slick from gore and entrails and brains. Straining every muscle and sinew in his body, he fought alongside the Templars.

Seasoned warriors that they were, the knights had leaped into their saddles mere moments after the Saracens had erupted through Blanche Garde's portcullis. The sergeants had similarly rushed to counterattack with pikes and maces and battle-axes. Holding aloft the black-and-white Beauseant that was both a banner and a beacon, they'd rushed to meet the unexpected assault.

Like Simon, every one of them was now drenched in so much blood and gore that it near obliterated the red crosses on the knights' surcoats and the black crosses on those of the sergeants.

Thank God and all the saints Sir Guy had ordered Avenger barded and saddled at the first signs of attack. A terrified Will Farrier had been gripping the destrier's reins with white, shaking hands when Simon had charged back to order a protective troop for Jocelyn. With a shouted command for Will to remain with Sir Guy, Simon had leaped from the palfrey he had commandeered in the king's camp and swung astride the heavily muscled warhorse.

In the desperate hours—or was it mere minutes?—since, Avenger had more than proved his mettle. Responding to the slightest pressure of Simon's knees, the bay wheeled, bit, kicked and trampled to devastating effect. Blood poured from wounds to its neck and haunches but the destrier proved as effective a weapon as any lance or sword.

Avenger evidenced even more value when Simon saw Bertrand de Tremelay go down. The Grand Master was surrounded by a half-dozen Saracen foot soldiers. One lunged forward to grab his mount's reins. Another ducked under his slashing sword and thrust his pike at the furiously battling knight. The force of the thrust pierced de Tremelay's mail and toppled him from the saddle.

"Templars!" The cry ripped from Simon's raw, smoke-seared throat. "To the Master!"

He spurred Avenger and used the barrel-chested courser as a battering ram to force a path through the swarming foot soldiers. De Tremelay was on his feet when Simon reached him. His right arm dangled uselessly at his side, but he'd transferred his sword to his left and now swung the blade in vicious arcs.

Simon did what he'd spent almost his entire life training to do. He killed and dismembered. Ruthlessly. Dispassionately. Swiftly. Within mere moments, the ground around the Grand Master was littered with corpses.

"I'll not forget this," de Tremelay shouted gratefully when Simon dismounted to help him back onto his courser.

They would be lucky if either of them lived to remember anything, Simon thought grimly as he dragged himself into the saddle again. The battle raged all around them. Vicious balls of fire still shot through the night sky.

As he plunged back into the fray, he could only pray that Jocelyn was sheltered and safe.

The battle was over by dawn.

Baldwin had rallied his forces and charged the army at his rear. Even before the queen and the rest of the camp heard that his desperate counterattack had succeeded, wild rumors as to who'd led the army that had attacked them swirled as thick as the smoke that hung like a pall over the battlefield.

Against all odds, the Templars had routed the attackers who'd poured out of Blanche Garde's gates. Then, incredibly, they'd battled their way to the gates themselves and stormed through them. The hilltop fortress was now back in Frankish hands.

But at horrific cost. When at last it was deemed safe for the queen to emerge from her protective position, she looked stricken to her very soul by the carnage around her. She stood with Jocelyn on one side, Lady Sibyl on the other, and surveyed the scene with red-rimmed eyes.

"Dear God above," she rasped in a smoke-ravaged whisper. "Will this kingdom ever know peace?"

For a moment she looked old beyond her years. So old and worn that Jocelyn put out a hand wrapped in bandages torn from her linen undertunic.

Melisande might be the daughter, wife and mother of kings, but she'd lived her entire life in a land torn by strife. She knew all too well the price that must be paid to hold this kingdom together. Drawing in a ragged breath, she squared her shoulders.

"We must needs find the king's marshal," she told Sir Guy. "He—or his second in command if Sir Humphrey has fallen—will organize succor for the wounded and identification of the dead. These ladies and I will assist how we may."

Jocelyn didn't have Lady Constance's skill at physiking the sick. As chatelaine of Fortemur, however, she'd seen her share of broken bones set and crushed limbs sawed off. Even so, the gruesome burns, weeping blisters and spilled entrails made her gag until at last she grew accustomed to such horrific human misery.

All the while she helped tend to the wounded, she wondered desperately whether Simon had survived the storming of Blanche Garde. She didn't learn his fate until the king came in search of his mother sometime past noon. By then every bone in Jocelyn's body ached with fatigue, and grime had etched its way in every fold of her skin.

Baldwin looked no better. Blood stained his surcoat. Soot rimmed his eyes. He'd lost his helm with its gold coronet and had shoved back his mailed hood to seek relief from the sun that now beat down mercilessly. But no sign of the enmity that had pitted mother against son in their fierce struggle for power showed in his face as he reached down to help the queen rise.

She put her hand in his and got stiffly to her feet. Her gaze raked his tired face as she sought verification of the rumors that were now all but fact.

"So it's true? It was the Emir of Damascus?"

Jocelyn held her breath. Several of the men she'd tended had sworn they'd recognized the emir's standard, but they could well have been mistaken in the dark of night and heat of battle.

"It was the emir," Baldwin confirmed heavily.

"Is he dead?"

"He is."

"May the bastard rot in hell!"

Just in time, Jocelyn bit back a heartfelt endorsement of the queen's wish. With so many dead and dying all around them, this was hardly the time to give vent to personal feelings. And truth be told, she was more concerned at this moment with Simon's fate than with the emir's.

"Come, Lady Mother." The king led her to the

palfrey he'd brought for her. "Blanche Garde is ours once more. I'll see you housed within its walls."

"Attend me, Lady Sibyl. You, also, Lady Jocelyn."

Baldwin held the reins while the queen mounted. Squires performed the same service for her ladies. While she settled into the saddle, Jocelyn made bold to address the king.

"Do you have word of Simon de Rhys?"

"Who?"

"The knight who commanded my guard. You sent him to tell the Templars to hold at all costs."

Wearily, the king shook his head. "I don't know his fate. We'll find out soon enough, however. The Grand Master has sent word that he awaits us inside the keep."

Corpses of both defender and attacker littered the steep incline leading to the castle's gates. Baking in the sun, many of the bodies were already black with flies. Added to that was the smoke from the still-smoldering funeral pyres. Jocelyn thought she'd become accustomed to the odor of death. Yet she had to draw her grimy sleeve over her nose and mouth to keep from retching.

Once inside the gates of Blanche Garde, the scene was somewhat less grim. Apparently the Saracens had surrendered shortly after the Templars had stormed the gates. They now had to be guarded from those who remained of the keep's original Latin population. Understandably, the survivors wanted to avenge their dead.

It soon became clear that the Templars had prevented their wholesale slaughter and enforced a rigid discipline. Jocelyn saw evidence of their work everywhere. Sergeants in the distinctive black tunics supervised work parties cleaning away the debris of battle. Clerical monks inscribed the names of the living and the dead. Cooks had the ovens fired. Even the Grand Master's own farrier was already at the bellows in the inner bailey, his face sweaty and red as he reshod warhorses that had thrown shoes during the battle.

But look as she might, Jocelyn caught no glimpse of Simon's tall form among the knights restoring order to the keep. Her throat got tighter and her heart weighed heavier as she trailed the king, his mother and their entourage into Blanche Garde's great hall.

A small gathering waited for them within. Two women stood off to one side, obviously summoned to attend the queen. The majority of the welcoming party, however, consisted of battle-stained warriors. The Grand Master of the Knights Templar stood at their head. Jocelyn recognized the thin, ascetic monk even before he detached himself from the group and came forward to greet Baldwin.

"Majesty."

"Brother de Tremelay."

The Templar cradled his bandaged right arm in his left as he and the king embraced. Only then did Jocelyn see the one she sought above all others.

"Simon!"

The glad cry burst from her before she could control it. The joy on Simon's face more than made up for her impetuous outburst. He took an involuntary step forward. Then, to Jocelyn's searing dismay, he caught himself.

His brow raised, Bertrand de Tremelay noted the knight's reaction, but the oaths the Grand Master had taken so many years ago bound him as fast as any chains. He would not—could not, according to the strict rules of his order—have discourse with women. Nor could he allow any of his acolytes to do so. But he'd been a man much longer than he'd been a monk. No stranger to human emotions, he directed his gaze to that of the queen.

Melisande intercepted the signal. She nodded once, a mere tilt of her head, and let a sigh slip from between her lips. "These horrific hours have sapped me more than I realized. I fear I must…" She sighed again and pressed the back of her hand to her grimy brow. "I truly must have rest."

Her son's face paled under its coating of dirt and gore. With a bite to his voice, he barked out an order to the two women who stood off to the side.

"Take the queen and her ladies to the women's

bower. I would that they might rest and cleanse themselves."

The two hurried forward and dropped into a curtsy before Melisande. They looked every bit as worn as the queen and the ladies who accompanied her. Jocelyn could only imagine what they might have endured while hostile forces occupied the keep. When the queen gave them leave to rise, the eldest of them issued a simple request.

"If you'll come with us, Majesty, we'll take you to the women's solar. Lady Alys awaits you there."

Before acquiescing, the queen turned to her son and issued a regal request. "I would ask that you come to me in due time so we might confer on the disposition of Blanche Garde."

"Send word when you are ready, Lady Mother."

Jocelyn hesitated. How could she quit the hall without exchanging so much as a word with Simon? As if reading her mind, Melisande paused a moment and gave him a weary smile.

"I would speak with you also, de Rhys. I will send for you later, after I've had time to confer with my son."

"Yes, Majesty."

His blue eyes went from Melisande to the woman beside her. Jocelyn hugged that brief glance to her breast as she trailed the queen and Lady Sybil from the great hall.

* * *

In the women's solar they were greeted by a lady and two young girls whose swollen, red-rimmed eyes told their own tale. The lady was Alys, wife to the lord who'd held Blanche Garde in the queen's name. She dropped into a deep curtsy and welcomed Melisande in a voice ragged with grief.

"Would that I could greet you in other circumstances, Majesty."

The queen took her hands and drew her to her feet. "What of your husband?"

"Dead. With our three sons. They…they fought to hold Blanche Garde most valiantly."

"I doubt it not," the queen said gently. "And you? Your daughters? Were you ill used?"

"No," the woman said wearily, "but we have not been allowed to leave this chamber. Tell me, how do the rest of our people fare?"

"Come, let us sit and I will tell you what I know."

The telling afforded Lady Alys little succor. Her neck bowed and her shoulders drooped with sorrow as the queen related the information she'd pieced together since the start of the attack. By the time she finished, Lady Alys and her daughters were awash in tears.

Jocelyn kept busy for the next few hours assisting Lady Sibyl in seeing to the queen's needs. Those included washing, eating, and ordering the personal possessions recovered from the camp. Luckily, several of the queen's trunks and chests had been stored in a separate tent and were found intact.

Once Melisande was rested, the queen sent word to her son that she was ready to speak with him. Before he arrived, she dismissed everyone from her presence.

Jocelyn used the respite to go in search of Simon. She wished desperately to hear from his own lips how he'd fared during the battle. To her bitter disappointment, she learned he'd ridden out with the Grand Master.

Frustrated, she sent pages in search of Sir Guy. Only after Sir Guy had confirmed that the men of Fortemur were being well cared for did she take time for herself. Thus she was robed in a borrowed gown with her hair freshly washed and rolled into a net when the queen sent a page with instructions that she desired the lady Jocelyn's presence.

The midafternoon sun blazed down mercilessly outside, but servants had draped oil-soaked cloths over the bower's windows to block the smoke and stench of the battlefield. The queen was seated at a sewing table inlaid with mother-of-pearl. She looked once again a queen in a bliaut of fern green trimmed with gold embroidery. The bright color did nothing to lighten her somber mood, however, as she gestured Jocelyn to the seat beside her.

"I have spoken with my son. Since Blanche Garde was part of my dower, it is mine to dispose of as I will. I have decided, and Baldwin concurs, that I should assign it to the Templars since it was they who saved the keep."

Jocelyn certainly couldn't disagree. Such a gift would only be a small measure of gratitude for saving both a king and a kingdom. Yet dread curled in her stomach. She sensed… Nay, she knew with unquestioned certainty where the queen was leading.

"The king says the Grand Master has nothing but praise for de Rhys. According to de Tremelay, he was at the front, right in the thick of things. He also says your knight saved his life."

Her knight. The choice of words tore at Jocelyn's heart as Melisande continued.

"And I, of course, can personally attest to his courage. The man saved my life, as well."

The horror of the night just past invaded the room and held both women in its cruel maw. Never, as long as she lived, would Jocelyn forget the sight of that fireball ripping through the queen's blue-and-silver tent. Or Simon, wreathed in flames, stumbling from what could well have been Melisande's funeral pyre. So she wasn't surprised to hear the queen had discussed suitable recompense.

"My son and I have discussed how to best reward

him. One option is to leave him here, in charge of Blanche Garde after I grant it to the Templars."

Jocelyn's chest contracted with equal parts pride and dismay. For a newly inducted Templar to be given such a charge was unheard of. Most had to serve a probationary period of a year or more, living as a humble, barefoot monk in a cloister when not fighting in the field.

That the queen and her son would so condition their gift of Blanche Garde was an incredible honor. And one that would steal Simon away from Jocelyn forever. Burying that base thought, she spoke from her heart.

"Such a reward is no more than he deserves, Majesty."

"I agree."

"Then…" She had to fight to keep the hollowness from her voice. "Then it's done."

"Mayhap," the queen said slowly. With a tilt of her head, she turned the subject. "Let us talk of you for a moment. We must needs still find you a husband."

"At least it won't be Ali ben Haydar!"

The retort slipped out before Jocelyn could stop it. The fierce satisfaction that came with it filled some of the hole in her heart.

"No," Melisande acknowledged with a twist of her lips. "It won't be Ali ben Haydar. My son informs me the emir's head now decorates a pike."

This time Jocelyn didn't even try to bite back her

fierce exclamation. "I hope the crows peck out the traitorous bastard's eyes!"

"So do I, girl. So do I."

Thus were the twisted politics of this much fought-over land, Jocelyn thought. Christian or Muslim, knight or king. It mattered not. They were allies one moment, enemies the next. Would it ever change?

In her heart of hearts, she feared it would not. A hundred, nay a thousand years from now blood would still stain these sands. Such was the nature of man that what one had, the other wanted. It was not faith that drove them, but power and wealth and riches.

As if in echo of her cynical thoughts, the queen heaved a tired sigh. "Now," she said heavily, "we must consider the emir's successor."

Jocelyn's head snapped back. Dear God and all the saints! Surely, surely, Baldwin and his mother did not still look to Damascus to help them hold their borders.

"Please," she begged. "Tell me you do not think to give me to one of the emir's sons."

The hesitation before the queen replied was so brief she might have almost imagined it. Almost.

"No, we don't think to give you to one of ben Haydar's sons. Those with any power have made it known their loyalties lie with Saladin."

And if they had not? Rebellion bubbled hot and furious in Jocelyn's veins. After all they'd been through, all they'd endured! She could not believe the queen would still use her as a pawn. Her mouth had set tight when Melisande put a finger under her chin and tipped her face to the light.

"Do not look daggers at me, child. I've not forgot what you and your knight did for me this past night." She waited for the words to sink in before continuing. "This de Rhys. He's more than proven himself worthy of you. And of Fortemur. We could give you to him."

Like a mace swung with all the force of a warrior's arm, surprise knocked every rebellious thought from Jocelyn's head.

"Majesty!"

The explosion of joy behind the breathless reply told the older woman all she needed to know. Sighing, Melisande released her chin.

"So it's as I thought. It was de Rhys who took your maidenhead, not Geoffrey de Lusignan."

There was no point in lying now.

"It's true. I did lay with him. Not by his choice, I must add."

When the queen lifted a startled brow, Jocelyn shrugged. She was beyond shame now.

"Simon was taken by pirates on his way to Outremer, Majesty. I purchased him in the slave market at El-Arish and offered him a choice. His freedom in exchange for one night in my bed."

"You did not!"

"I did."

"And he agreed to this infamous bargain?"

"Reluctantly."

The queen regarded her with no little surprise and shock for a moment longer, then burst into laughter. "Ah, lady. I'll wager he shed his reluctance with his trews."

An answering grin tugged at Jocelyn's lips. "Indeed he did."

For a brief moment, they were just two women sharing the kind of jest only another female could appreciate. All too soon their merriment faded, and Melisande's expression grew serious.

"I would have this matter settled before I return to Jerusalem. Do you want de Rhys, or no?"

"I do." The admission came without thought or hesitation from deep within Jocelyn's innermost being. "I long for him more with every breath I take."

Like a shimmering desert oasis, the idea that she might wed Simon hovered in her mind. She clung to it for precious seconds, letting it fill every corner of her soul. She could see them walking Fortemur's ramparts together. Discussing what percentage of the taxes should go to defense and what to Yule or Easter entertainments for her people. Celebrating the birth of strong sons, loving daughters. Then, like the illusions that led many a desert traveler to despair, the tantalizing visions turned to dust.

"I want him," she said with a raw ache in her chest, "but I can't ask him to forswear himself."

Melisande blinked in surprise. Clearly she hadn't expected this response.

"Are you speaking of his pledge to join the Templars?" she asked. "That's easily enough remedied. I will talk to my son and have him inform the Grand Master that—"

"Please, do not."

Throwing herself out of her chair, Jocelyn knelt at the queen's feet. She'd disappointed Sir Hugh. She'd used Simon ruthlessly to her own deceitful ends. She would not, could not, allow the queen and her son to do the same.

"De Rhys holds his honor above all else. It's what makes him the man he is. I would not take that from him."

The queen's face softened. Sighing, she looked long into her ward's eyes. "Are you sure, girl? This is your life we speak of, and his."

Jocelyn didn't look away. "I'm sure."

Melisande didn't speak for several moments. She had to have guessed how much those two simple words had cost. Sympathy swam in her eyes as she stroked Jocelyn's cheek. Then, as they must, the heavy burdens she'd lived with all her life came to the fore.

"The collapse of our alliance with Damascus makes it imperative that we find you another husband, girl, and fast. One strong enough to hold Fortemur against attack."

Jocelyn accepted the dictum without flinching. She, too, shouldered heavy responsibilities.

"I agree, Majesty."

"Thank the saints," Melisande murmured with the beginnings of a rueful smile. "I feared another battle royal."

"All I ask is that you make him a Frankish knight."

"After all we've endured together, it's little enough to ask of me. You have my word."

Jocelyn could only pray that she would hold to it.

Chapter Twelve

Unbeknownst to Jocelyn, Simon was having much the same conversation at almost the same moment.

The setting for their talks was different. Instead of a dim chamber shielded from the stench of death by oiled clothes and fragrant candles, Simon and Bertrand de Tremelay circled the base of Blanche Garde's chalky cliffs in the blazing heat of late afternoon.

Sweat ran in rivulets down the Grand Master's thin face. Despite his broad shoulders and muscular thighs, his years showed in the graying hair plastered to his skull and the deep grooves etched into his lean cheeks. The arm that had taken the vicious lance thrust was now bandaged tight across his chest. Another bandage circled his thigh.

De Tremelay didn't give so much as a passing nod to his wounds, however. He was a warrior to his bones. As well Simon should know. Hadn't he witnessed firsthand the Grand Master's refusal to beg for quarter even when surrounded by a half-dozen or more Saracens?

Yet the past few minutes had revealed an all-too-human side to Bertrand de Tremelay. Not to mention the man's unabashed ambition on behalf of his order. Even now glee and more than a hint of avarice colored his voice as he reiterated the astounding news he'd imparted some moments ago.

"I'll tell you again, de Rhys, you performed an incomparable service for the Knights Templar when you rescued the queen from that blazing tent. The king could scarce hold himself in check when he spoke of it. That Baldwin and his mother would cede Blanche Garde to our order is a feather in my cap. That they would insist I leave you in charge is most assuredly one in yours."

"I'm honored, sir, and humbled."

"As well you should be. Our order boasts many knights far senior to you who would jump at the chance to govern such a magnificent holding. I will confess I told the king so, but he remained adamant. For all their differences, Baldwin and his mother think with one mind on many issues."

When the Grand Master's intense, penetrating gaze swept the fortress set atop its white cliffs, Simon's followed. Despite his protestation of unworthiness, an undeniable stir of pride swirled deep in his chest.

Never in his wildest imaginings had he envisioned commanding such a mighty keep.

Unbidden, an image of Fortemur's turrets and towers leaped into his head. With it came one of its mistress, with her silver-blond hair tossed by the wind and her face aglow as she watched her peregrine falcon ride the air currents. Hard on the heels of those forbidden thoughts came others, even more insidious.

Could he trade one fortress for another?

One vow for another?

Now that the emir's treachery and death had destroyed hopes of an alliance with Damascus, Melisande and her son would give Jocelyn to another husband. Why not to him? He'd saved the queen from sure death, had helped the Grand Master escape the Saracens who had brought him down. They both considered him worthy enough to take command of Blanche Garde, as did the king.

Perhaps they would give him Fortemur and its lady instead.

A muscle jumped in the side of Simon's jaw as he broached the possibility slowly, carefully. "Father, may I speak with you of a personal matter?"

The Grand Master dragged his glance from the towering walls. "Of course."

"When I left home, my sire lay dying of the wasting sickness. He had not the strength left to do penance for his sins and pressed me to do it for him. To that end, I acceded to his earnest entreaty that I join the Knights Templar."

"Do you say you vowed to join our order to redeem your father's soul?"

"What was left of it to be redeemed."

De Tremelay considered that for several moments before he shook his head. "No man can purchase salvation for someone else, nor release another soul from purgatory."

"That's what the Bishop of Clairvaux told me."

"The bishop is a wise and saintly man. He told you correctly."

"But he also said that if the sinner is truly repentant, any good acts he did—or others did in his name—can earn him indulgences."

"That's so, if he does indeed repent. Tell me, did your sire confess his sins?"

"He said he did."

"Was he given absolution?"

"As far as I know."

"Well, then. It sounds as though he was truly repentant, but I will tell you this, de Rhys. God alone is the judge of what penalty we all must pay for our sins."

Deep in thought, de Tremelay lifted his gaze to the castle walls again.

"I would say, though, that what you've done here will have won your sire at least a Plenary Indulgence.

By holding to your vow, you'll spare him—and yourself—even more time in purgatory."

"What if I don't hold to it?"

The Grand Master's head whipped around. "Why would you not?"

The muscle in Simon's jaw twitched again. He could feel it jump as he met a hard, penetrating stare.

"I'm not suited to Holy Orders, Your Grace. There's a woman. A lady. I crave her above all else."

"Ahhh."

De Tremelay raked a mailed fist through his sweat-flattened hair. His thin face creased in a knowing smile.

"Men have lusted for women since Adam first laid eyes on Eve. It's the natural order of things. What God has ordained for us. Why do you think our order has such strict rules? Why we may not so much as speak to, much less have congress with, any female? Only by avoiding all such contact can we rise above the weakness of our mortal flesh and dedicate ourselves to a higher purpose."

Simon had only to recall his stolen hours with Jocelyn to know he would never rise above the weakness she engendered in him.

"God's will sent you to Outremer, de Rhys, and you've but begun to fulfill your destiny here. One as strong of heart and arm as you are will rise quickly within our order. I see great things ahead for you."

He flung out an arm in a gesture that encompassed a wide sweep of chalky hill and forested land. “You’ve brought Blanche Garde to the Knights Templar. You will bring us more. I’m sure of it.”

Simon was no fool. He knew politics and avarice played as much within the Church as without. The order of the Knights Templar might have sprung from the noble intention of protecting pilgrims on their way to the Holy Land, but its tentacles now reached far beyond these shores. Their holdings in Europe and Byzantium rivaled those of kings and emperors. So did their treasury. It was rumored the Templars’ chief of the exchequer had loaned so great a sum to Louis of France to finance his ill-fated Crusade that the king must needs beggar his entire kingdom to discharge the debt.

Now, because of the actions of the landless son of a minor knight, they had the chance to add another major keep to their holdings. Despite the debt of gratitude de Tremelay claimed he owed to Simon, he would not willingly release him from his vow. Not if it meant losing such a rich prize as Blanche Garde.

As if in echo of his grim thoughts, the older man straightened in the saddle and took up his reins.

“You will have time and more to purge yourself of all carnal thoughts during your fasting and abasement prior to induction, de Rhys. Because you’ve already proved yourself in battle and brought such honor to our order, I can shorten the time required for these rituals. You'll face a trial of only days instead of weeks. And I am confident that five days hence you will don the white surcoat of a Templar, and all things will find their proper place in your heart."

Simon didn't share his conviction. What he felt for Jocelyn was so different from what he'd felt for any other woman. This aching need went beyond lust, beyond all thoughts of wealth or power. Beyond honor.

Yet he'd come so far. Endured so much to reach this point. He owed it to himself—and to Jocelyn—to take this final test. He would submit to purification rituals. Abase himself both physically and mentally. Open his heart, as the Grand Master urged. And five days hence, he would know without any hesitation which path to tread.

"I understand the wisdom in what you say," he acknowledged, "and will obey."

"Good. Now let us return to the keep so I may organize your induction."

Sheer chance brought them to Blanche Garde's outer gate just as a troop wearing the red and black of Fortemur clattered across the drawbridge. Jocelyn rode at its head, Sir Guy beside her. Those of her men who'd survived the vicious battle of the night before followed. In the midst of their ranks, two drays pulled a cart conveying tightly bound bundles. The size and shape of the bundles told Simon they could only be Fortemur's dead.

Bound by his vows, the Grand Master could do no more than nod to the woman leading the troop. Simon was not yet subject to such restraint.

"Lady Jocelyn!"

She drew rein, her gaze locked with his. She'd washed the grime from her face and changed into clean garments, but her voice was still hoarse from the smoke.

"I looked for you," she said with a smile that didn't quite reach her eyes. "The queen told me that she will grant Blanche Garde to the Templars in recognition of their heroic acts. And that you are to be given command of the keep. I wanted to let you know how happy I am for you, Simon. Such an honor is no more than you deserve."

He nodded but was more concerned with the weariness in both her voice and her face at this moment than the disposition of the keep. "You're so tired you can scarce sit your saddle. Why do you depart before you have rested at least through the night?"

"I'll not leave Sir Hugh and the others of Fortemur to be burned or tossed into a mass grave." Her throat working, she cast a glance over her shoulder at the shrouded bodies. "I must take them home for burial."

"Tomorrow," he urged. "Take them tomorrow."

Temptation rose so thick and hot in Jocelyn's

throat she near choked on it. He would never know how fiercely she'd debated leaving Blanche Garde, or how strenuously Sir Guy had argued against it. Nor could he know how much she ached to stay just one more night. If she did, she could slip away with him to some dark, secret corner. Rest her head on his shoulder. Ease some of the horror of the night just past in his arms.

And then? Would she whisper to him of the queen's extraordinary offer? Would she weep and cling and beg him yet again to break the vow he'd sworn before man and God?

She would. She knew without a shadow of a doubt that she would. And when she did, she would only add to the misery engulfing them both. Better to cut all ties now, while Simon still retained his honor and she a shred of dignity.

Yet the parting was so much harder than she'd ever imagined it could be. Especially when he nudged his mount closer to hers and reached over to take her hand.

"Mayhap it's for the best. As you say, Sir Hugh and the other men of Fortemur deserve burial in hallowed ground. And all of you will sleep better away from this stench. I have business to attend to here yet, but—"

He broke off, his jaw working. He could not say more, she knew. What was there to say?

"God keep you safe, Simon. I pray you find joy in the life you're about to enter."

Holding her eyes with his, he raised her hand and brushed his lips across the back. Once. Twice.

"I pray so, too, lady."

The Templars' secret induction rituals had already given rise to many a rumor among other churchmen and laity alike. Kings and barons speculated openly about the ceremony. Commoners whispered of it behind closed doors. Even the Pope himself had supposedly written to a previous Grand Master to inquire about it.

If so, the reply must needs have been vague at best. As Simon was informed when two brother knights stripped him, every inductee must swear on pain of death and the loss of his immortal soul never to reveal what transpired in the hours and days to come.

"Do you so swear?" the Grand Master demanded, his eyes burning above the snowy white of his surcoat.

"I do."

"Then kneel, de Rhys, and empty your head of all thoughts but the glory of God."

Simon dropped to his knees on hard stone covered with a woven straw mat. It was late. Well past midnight. The main doors to the chapel were locked from the inside. The entrances to the choir loft and the private balcony where the lord and lady of the keep would hear Mass were similarly sealed. The flicker of candles set at intervals along the nave did little to dispel the gloom.

Blanche Garde's chapel had sustained considerable damage during the keep's occupation by the Saracens. The cross that had previously hung above the marble altar had been ripped from its mounting and burnt to a pile of gray ash. The gem-studded chalice and precious cloth of gold altar scarf that had reportedly been gifts of Queen Melisande herself were missing and had not yet been recovered. Even the marble sarcophagi lining the alcoves on either side of the nave bore the scars of assault by mace or battle-ax.

Despite the obvious signs of desecration, an air of sanctity pervaded the still, shadow-filled chapel. Perhaps it was the intensity of the knight-priests who stood to either side of Simon. Or the expression on the face of the Grand Master when he addressed the potential inductee.

"You will neither eat nor drink anything save water nor speak to any living soul until you have completed the tasks we require of you. Do you understand?"

"I do."

"Here, then, is your first task."

De Tremelay held out a long-handled flail. When the hooked barbs at the ends of its dozen or more tails clinked against one another, the small sounds echoed in Simon's ears like lost souls crying to each other.

"You will scourge yourself thrice hourly from

now until dawn," de Tremelay instructed grimly. "Betimes, you will beg Christ to make you worthy of His grace."

Everything in Simon cringed at the prospect of flailing his still-raw back with the vicious barbs, but he accepted the whip without comment. He'd chosen this path. Pledged his oath before God and man. He would not shy from it now.

"We will return for you at dawn," de Tremelay said. "At that time, I will assign the next of your tasks."

He signaled to the two knights. Their footsteps echoed in the dim emptiness as they made for the chapel door. A heavy key clanked in the lock. The wooden door creaked open on iron hinges, swung shut. The grate of the key in the lock again sounded as loud as a clap of thunder to Simon's ears.

When the echo died, he drew a long, shuddering breath and tightened his fist on the handle of the flail.

Chapter Thirteen

Fortemur lay only a little more than twelve leagues to the west of Blanche Garde, but the path climbed steep hills and wound through vineyards and orchards before beginning a slow descent to the sea.

Because they'd departed so late, Jocelyn and her troop were forced to spend the night on the road. Sir Guy requisitioned a bed for her in the home of an olive merchant. She slept but fitfully and roused early to continue the journey. By noon of the next day, she could see the Mediterranean shimmering in the far distance.

She near wept when she rode through Fortemur's massive gates the next afternoon. This was home. This place was safe. Now, at least, she wouldn't have to exchange it for the marble fountains and perfumed gardens of the emir's harem.

Before parting from Melisande, she'd wrung

a reluctant promise from the queen. Both women acknowledged Jocelyn must wed, and soon. Given the emir's treachery and the certainty of further battles to come, it was more imperative than ever that Fortemur be vested in a knight strong enough to defend it against attack. A Frankish knight, Melisande had agreed. One who would hold Fortemur for the crown. As Simon would have held it, Jocelyn thought with a stab of pain so sharp it near tumbled her from her saddle.

No! She couldn't allow herself to dwell on what might have been. There were graves to be dug. Widows to grieve with. Children to comfort. Still, she almost fell into Lady Constance's welcoming arms and had to fight to hold back her tears when she related the astounding events at Blanche Garde to Thomas of Beaumont and his pinch-faced wife.

"I would have come to your relief myself," the king's cousin asserted officiously. "But with Hugh and Guy both most anxious to answer your call, I felt it my duty to hold Fortemur against possible attack."

She was too sick at heart to do more than nod. "There's much to do. Let's get to it."

The days passed swiftly. The nights seemed endless.

Exhausted though she was from the ordeal at Blanche Garde and the grim tasks she had to complete on her return, Jocelyn tossed restlessly in bed and woke more weary than when she'd retired. When she did drift into sleep, her dreams were all too often of blood and fire and the pain Simon must even now be enduring.

She knew no more than anyone else of the trials an aspirant to the Order of the Knights Templar must go through. She'd heard rumors, however. Whispers. Gruesome tales. How could he endure them after all he'd suffered at the hands of his captors?

Tortured by horrific imaginings, she thrust aside the bed coverings and padded on bare feet to the intricately carved prie-dieu. Her hands went white at the knuckles as she bowed her head and pleaded with God to spare Simon what agony He could.

Night bled into day.

Day darkened to night.

When two brother knights dragged Simon from the chapel, he'd long since lost all sense of time or self. It was true, he thought hazily as they scrubbed the blood and sweat from his naked body. Deliberate, torturous self-abasement could indeed erase all carnal thoughts. Pain could take a person beyond the realm of the physical.

He could scarce recall his own name, much less the one he'd thought would remain emblazoned forever on his heart. It was only with the sheerest effort of will that he was able to raise his arms so the brother knights might clothe him with clean, rough-spun garments.

They let him eat then. Two dry crusts of bread. One slice from a cheese wheel. He crammed them into his mouth like a pig at the trough and washed them down with watered wine.

"Slowly," one of them murmured sympathetically. "Drink slowly, else your shrunken belly will heave and churn and spew everything up."

Simon acknowledged the wisdom of this advice some moments later, when his roiling belly threatened to do just that. Drawing on his last, tattered shreds of will, he managed to choke back the acrid taste of bile. The knight beside him nodded in approval.

"If you're ready, the Grand Master awaits."

"I'm ready," he croaked.

It was dark, he noted as they led him once again to the chapel. Nigh onto midnight, he guessed, although the fog swirling inside his head made a mockery of his thoughts. This time he was halted just outside the door.

"Knock thrice," the knight holding him up with a firm grip instructed.

Thrice. That pierced the whirling haze. Once for the Father, once for the Son, once for the Holy Ghost. Breathing hard, he did as instructed.

"Who's without?" a voice boomed from inside.

"An aspirant to our order," his escort replied.

"Bring him to me."

His heart hammering, Simon entered. Was it just an hour ago he'd exited the chapel? Mere moments since he'd yielded all to pain and darkness?

The mat he'd knelt and slept and wept on was gone. All trace of blood and vomit and excrement had disappeared. A hundred, nay, a thousand, wax candles dispelled the darkness that had surrounded him. Their fragrance joined that of the incense that sent spirals of scented smoke curling from silver dishes.

Those of the Templars who'd survived the battle stood in two rows. They flanked the Grand Master, who gestured Simon's escort to take his place beside his brothers in arms.

Without the man's supporting hand, Simon near toppled to the stone floor. He caught himself in time. His breath hissing through locked jaws, he straightened. In the distant corner of his mind not hazed by pain, he noted the attendant standing just beyond de Tremelay.

Was that a skull in the man's hands, cut off and inverted to form a bowl? Sweet Lord, was the dark liquid in the bowl blood? The tales Simon had heard of aspirants required to seal their oaths by drinking the blood of enemies spun through his dazed mind as the Grand Master made a short, chopping gesture with his sword.

"State your name, that all may hear who aspires to join our ranks."

"I am—" He had to stop and lick his lips. His throat raw, he began again. "I am Simon de Rhys."

"Hear me, de Rhys." De Tremelay's eyes burned with intensity as he leaned in. "You've now had a taste of the rigors every Templar must endure. Our life is one of hardship, not ease. Danger, not indulgence. If you join our ranks, you will sigh for sleep. Pray for a wormy crust of bread or flask of water. You will own nothing. Not the sword you wield in battle, nor your horses, nor your armor. All you bring with you, all you win by the strength of your arm, will belong to the order."

De Tremelay leaned closer. His voice reverberated with the passion of one who'd endured all the hardships he'd just enumerated.

"You will be loyal to no country," he continued. "No liege. Only to the Pope, the master of this order, and the brothers senior to you in rank. Do you understand what is asked of you?"

"Yes."

"Then answer now, before these witnesses. Are you in good health?"

For a stunned moment, Simon thought the man toyed with him. He stared at him stupidly and tried desperately to scrape the cobwebs from his mind. Only belatedly did he realize that de Tremelay was not referring to the wounds inflicted at his specific order.

"I'm in good health."

He had to force his reply past jaws near locked with pain.

"Are you in debt?"

"No."

"Are you betrothed, or married?"

For a moment, a mere heartbeat, the image of a pale-haired maiden pushed through the haze still fogging Simon's mind.

"No."

He couldn't be sure in his weakened state, but it seemed the Grand Master let out a low hiss of satisfaction.

"Do you belong to any other order?"

"No."

"Then we come to the final question. Tell me this, de Rhys, and tell me true. Do you take the oath of Knight Templar with a pure heart?"

Chapter Fourteen

Still Jocelyn could not sleep. She arose each morning before the dawn and applied herself so relentlessly to her duties as chatelaine that Fortemur's residents took to sliding away at her approach for fear of being set to yet another backbreaking task.

They couldn't escape her vigilant eye. She ordered the dovecotes cleaned and fresh rushes cut for every floor of the keep. Tapestries were taken down, beat with branches to remove their dust, and laboriously rehung. The beekeeper, the stable master and the ale master were all taken to account for vital tasks left too long undone.

Her ladies Jocelyn set to sewing several new gowns for the wedding she advised them would take place as soon as the queen or her son named a replacement groom. Sir Thomas's ferret-faced wife plied her needle along with them.

"Who will it be, do you think?" she asked when Jocelyn came to inspect their progress.

"I don't know."

Nor did she care. The passion that had driven her to take such outrageous risks to avoid marriage to Ali ben Haydar seemed to have drained away. She had the queen's promise that she would be given to a Frankish lord. Nothing else seemed to matter anymore.

"From all reports, Lord Eustace will soon have need of a bride." Thomas's wife knotted her thread and snipped it with the scissors attached to her belt. "His lady is rumored to lie on her deathbed. Maybe the queen will give you to him and join your holdings with his."

"Surely not!" Lady Constance protested sharply. "Eustace's bones creak even more than mine. He has to have celebrated seventy name days, if he's celebrated one."

"I doubt it not." A small, spiteful smile crossed the other woman's face. "But what matters age when kingdoms are at stake?"

What matter, indeed? Blowing out a ragged breath, Jocelyn spun on her heel and left the women to their stitching.

To distract herself from fruitless speculation, she threw herself with ever more energy into inspecting and shoring up Fortemur's defenses. Her ceaseless efforts took so much from her that she grew more haggard and short-tempered with each hour. Finally Sir Guy pleaded with his wife to intercede. Lady Constance did so in her blunt manner.

"By all that is holy, Jocelyn! You're driving us all to dip deep into the wine barrel. Take your falconer, your bird and your foul temper, and for God's sake quit the keep for a while."

It was, Jocelyn realized an hour later, just the antidote she needed for her ill humors. Sunshine and a bracing breeze off the sea cleared the last, lingering horror of Blanche Garde from her mind. The grace of her peregrine as it rode the updrafts with effortless ease gave her a measure of peace she never thought she would find again.

She couldn't help but think of the first time she had watched it fly. Simon had ridden with her to these same cliffs. Then, as now, the peregrine had demonstrated its sharp-taloned skills. And when it was done, she had taken Simon to the crystal cave.

Memories of that stolen hour filled her mind. She could almost feel his flesh against hers. Taste again the salt on his skin. He'd given her a gift she could only now appreciate, she realized. Not just carnal knowledge, nor yet a woman's searing, panting satisfaction. He'd given her the gift of love.

It would stay with her always. Whosoever she wed, wheresoever she went, she would hold the memory of their brief time together in a corner of her heart as special and private as her cave. She rested her leather-sheathed wrists on the pommel and watched the bird soar. The sight didn't completely erase the ache inside her, but the faint tinkle of the bells tethered to its leg did seem to soothe some of the sharp edges.

Would that she could fly with such unutterable grace, she thought with a sigh. Where would she go? Jerusalem, she thought. It would be wondrous indeed to view the holy sites from such a lofty perspective. Or Venice, perhaps. She'd heard tales of the palatial villas crowding its fog-shrouded waterways. Or—

"Mistress!"

Her falconer's shout jerked her from thoughts of canals and palaces. She would go nowhere, Jocelyn acknowledged, even as her mind leaped to the possibility of a threat. She was Fortemur. Her destiny lay now and always between its crenellated walls.

"What do you see?" she asked sharply.

"Look!"

She twisted in the saddle and saw that he pointed to a lone rider descending the road toward Fortemur. He was slumped in the saddle and too far away for her to see his face, but there was no mistaking those broad shoulders or Avenger's distinctive barding.

Everything in her went still. For long moments she couldn't squeeze so much as a breath from her lungs. A thousand chaotic thoughts tumbled through her mind. Why had Simon returned? Had he failed his initiation? Taken some grievous hurt?

What did it matter? He was here! Like one prodded from a trance by the sharp tip of a spear, she shouted a command at her escort.

"To me!"

Her heels dug into her mount's sides. Heart pounding, Jocelyn wove through the stunted trees lining the cliffs and thundered up the slope.

Simon dismounted slowly and waited while she threw herself from the saddle. His arms came around her with a fierceness that crushed the air from her lungs. Heedless of the men charging up the road after her, she thrust up on her toes to cover his mouth, his cheeks, even his chin with greedy kisses.

He returned them before burying his face in her hair. His hold was so tight she was sure her ribs would crack. Laughing, gasping, near sobbing with joy, she tried to ease back.

"Simon! I beg you. Let me draw a breath, then tell me what you do here!"

He gave a small grunt and loosed his grip. Only then did she realize he wasn't holding her so much as using her to hold himself up.

And his face! Sweet Lord, his face! Now that she could see past her tears of joy, the sight of him shocked her to her very core. He was so gaunt. So drawn and gray. His eyes, once as blue and bright as the sky itself, were dull and rimmed with red.

"Simon! Are you ill? Have you taken a—?"

She broke off when he lurched against her. Wrapping both arms around his waist, she staggered under his weight and cried to her men to give her aid. It took three of them to support him.

"Lay him in the grass beside the road," Jocelyn ordered frantically. "One of you go now, and fast! Fetch Sir Guy. Have him bring a wagon. And Lady Constance. Tell her—"

"No." The protest was little more than a rustle of air from between Simon's gritted teeth. "I can…ride. Help me…back ahorse."

Since his knees had given way and he was dragging those supporting him to the dirt, Jocelyn paid no heed to the ridiculous request.

"Do as I bid," she snapped at her men. "Lay him there." Whirling, she stabbed a finger at one of the others. "Get you to the keep."

The groan that ripped from Simon's throat when they stretched him out on the stubby grass stopped Jocelyn's breath in her throat. She dropped to her knees beside him. Her hands trembled so badly she couldn't loosen his mailed hood or shove it back from his sweat-drenched forehead.

"Can you speak, Simon? Tell me where you hurt."

His red, crusted lids lifted. For the merest instant,

a faint gleam pierced the dull glaze in his eyes and the ghost of a smile pulled at his lips.

"Where...do...I...not?"

"This is worse than before. Much worse."

Lady Constance's grim assessment sliced like a sword through the stillness pervading Jocelyn's bedchamber. Her hands were gentle as she bathed Simon's naked form, but her face wore a most grave expression.

"I've never seen such grievous wounds." She tossed the sodden, bloody rag into a bucket filled with reddened water and stretched out an imperious hand. "Give me another cloth."

Jocelyn jumped to do her bidding. She'd hovered at the older woman's side ever since her men had hauled Simon up the stairs and into her bed. A half-dozen others hovered nearby, ready and willing to give aid. Another of her ladies was among them. Two maids. A page poised to run and fetch as commanded. Two beefy men-at-arms to help lift and turn.

Sir Guy was there, too. As was Sir Thomas. The king's cousin pulled at his sparse red whiskers and asked yet again the question still burning in Jocelyn's mind.

"Why is he here?"

"I don't know."

"Has he brought a missive from the king?"

"We found no missive among his garments," she bit out.

"That's another thing. Why was he wearing the stained tunic he left Fortemur in? Didn't you tell me he was preparing for induction into the Order of the Knights Templar when you departed Blanche Garde?"

She gritted her teeth, praying for patience, and nodded.

"Then he should have been wearing the Templars' white mantle and red cross," Sir Thomas pointed out unnecessarily. "Unless he failed the tests," he added scornfully. "It's often so with men as big as this one. They present a fearsome appearance but cannot endure the most trivial—"

"You don't know of what you speak," Guy interrupted fiercely. Newly appointed by Jocelyn to fill Sir Hugh's position as castellan, he didn't bother to disguise his disdain for the king's cousin. "I was with de Rhys at Blanche Garde. I saw firsthand his bravery on the field."

"Oh, so? Well, all I can say is that he doesn't look brave now. He looks like some oaf flayed by his master for stealing a pig or—"

"Get out!"

Jocelyn whirled on him, her hands curling into claws. She'd had enough—more than enough!—of this blood-sucking leech.

"Get out of my chamber and out of my keep!"

Thomas stumbled back a step, his jaw dropping in sheer surprise. "What do you say?"

"You heard me. I want you gone within the hour. You and your whey-faced wife."

"You…you cannot order us away," he stammered. "Baldwin himself appointed me steward of Fortemur."

"I am *un*appointing you." Fire and fear for Simon blazed in equal measures in her heart. "Sir Guy, escort this man from my sight."

"Gladly."

Her new castellan hustled the indignant and still stuttering knight to the chamber's door. Had she given the matter a second thought, Jocelyn wouldn't have doubted King Baldwin would support this summary dismissal. He, like the queen, knew full well the timely arrival of Fortemur's troops had helped to turn the tide of battle. They owed her almost as much as they owed Simon.

That brought her back full square to the question still burning in her mind. Why was he here?

She got her answer late that night.

She'd abandoned all pretense and refused to leave Simon's side. She no longer gave a groat who knew he was in her bed, or that she ached with her whole being to join him there.

She couldn't slide in beside him, of course. His wounds were too grievous to risk aggravating them.

All she could do was banish everyone but Lady Constance from the chamber and pull a stool close so she might stroke his bruised and battered hand.

Minutes crawled by. Hour dragged into hour. Constance gave way to weariness and slumped in the chair she'd placed on the far side of the bed. On the verge of utter despair, Jocelyn laid her head on her crossed arms.

"You are…the sun…"

The hoarse whisper jerked her head up. Hope leaped like a dancing unicorn in her heart.

"Simon!"

Her glad cry brought Lady Constance bolting upright. So thrilled were both women to see him awake and his eyes clear that they near missed the words he added on a soughing breath.

"…that ends…my darkness."

Jocelyn whipped her gaze from him to Lady Constance and back again. She'd heard those words before. But where? When?

It burst on her of a sudden. The troubadour, Blondin, had sung that very line in the great hall, strumming his mandolin all the while. And just as quick, the full verse scrolled through her head.

Your whisper brightens my heart.
Your kiss feeds my soul.
You are the sun that ends my darkness.
I will be faithful to you forever,
In this life and the next.

Dear God! *This life and the next?*

The fear that Simon had dragged himself into the saddle and made the tortuous journey to Fortemur only to bid her farewell clutched at her heart like a mailed fist and squeezed so hard she couldn't draw a single breath. If not for Lady Constance's tart comment, she might have crumpled to the rushes into a sobbing, shapeless mass.

"So, de Rhys. You've decided to rejoin the living."

"Indeed I...have, lady." With an effort that was painful to watch, he smiled. "In more...ways than one."

That slow curve of his lips arrowed straight to Jocelyn's heart. "Simon," she said with a catch in her voice. "Please, please tell me. Why have you returned to Fortemur?"

"To...take you...to wife."

Chapter Fifteen

Simon's wounds healed more slowly this time than they had previously.

Jocelyn could only wonder how he'd found the strength to endure such obvious agony. Each time she thought on what he must have gone through, she wavered between fury and pride.

"I did it for you," he told her when at last he was able to rise from her bed and bathe. "For us."

She'd had pages haul buckets of heated water to fill the wooden tub. It was large enough for Jocelyn and at least two of her ladies to fit comfortably on bathing day. Simon fit, too, although he had to bend his knees almost to his chin to be accommodated.

Jocelyn had dismissed the pages. Told the maid to leave her bucket of soap and quit the chamber, as well. His recovery was new enough that she wanted this time with him for herself alone.

"And the Grand Master?" she asked, dipping a cloth into the soft soap. "Does he agree you are no longer bound by your vow to join the Templars?"

"I fulfilled my vow. I took every step required of me to join the order. What I could not do was lie before God, the Grand Master and my fellow knights."

That's all he would tell her. All else that occurred at Blanche Garde, apparently, would remain shrouded forever in secrecy.

"Oh, Simon." Gently, carefully, she washed arms and a chest so lacerated it near made her weep. "Could you not have reached this decision before you were subjected to such torture?"

"No, Jocelyn. I had to go through the induction rituals." His mouth curved above his soapy chest. "They were a small enough price to pay for the Lady of Fortemur."

"Ha! I would guess the fact that you convinced the queen to confirm her gift of Blanche Garde to the Templars whether you took command of it or not had as much to do with the fact that you're here as aught else."

"I suspect you're right." His smiled widened. "The Grand Master didn't draw a whole breath until Melisande put her seal to the documents."

That he could grin and make light of the ordeal that had come close to killing him almost robbed her of speech.

Almost.

Thoroughly incensed on his behalf, she was preparing to tell him what she thought of such machinations when he leaned back against the tub and regarded her through the screen of his sun-tipped lashes.

"Enough of the queen and the Grand Master. I would speak of us."

She sank onto her heels and let the cloth dangle from her hands.

"What's left to say? You've already informed me that you returned to Fortemur to take me to wife. I have to assume the queen and her son agreed to the match."

"They did."

"So?"

He reached for her hand and lifted it, cloth and all. His lips brushed the inside of her wrist with a kiss that made her pulse leap like a startled palfrey.

"So, lady, will you have me?"

"You know I will."

He dropped another kiss on her wrist. A smile played at the corners of his mouth, but above it his eyes were grave.

"I bring you nothing, Jocelyn. Not so much as a groat that I may call my own."

"Do you think I care?"

"You may not, but I do."

Men! They would ever measure their worth by the dram.

Her heart full to overflowing, she surged up on her knees. "I'll tell you what you bring me, Simon de Rhys. A strong arm I know will ever protect me. A heart so pure it would not, could not, violate an oath once given. You bring me joy, as well, and laughter and the most damnable lust. It fills every part of me," she confessed with a grimace. "I can't tell you how I ache for you to regain your strength enough to sate it."

He gave a bark of laughter. The rich sound filled the chamber even as he tightened his grip on her wrist.

"Ah, sweeting, I've regained enough strength for that."

"What are you…? No!"

Her shriek of protest got swamped by a mighty splash as he pulled her into the tub. Legs flailing, she flopped about like a speared sturgeon before he righted her.

"Are you mad?" She spit out a mouthful of soapy water. "Out of your head from pain?"

"Truth be told, I'm feeling better by the moment."

Since his hand had burrowed beneath her sodden skirts, Jocelyn could not but take him at his word. And when he shifted her so she straddled his hips, she felt even more insistent evidence of his recovery.

Terrified that she would add to his hurts, she tried to wiggle away off his lap.

"This is idiocy, Simon! You'll injure yourself."

"No, sweet Jocelyn, I won't. But for the love of God and all the saints, be still!"

The incident in the bathing tub convinced Jocelyn that Simon had recovered enough to exchange vows with her. Determined to see the deed done as quickly as possible, she harried Father Joseph into posting the banns that very afternoon. Then she shocked him with her insistence they need only remain nailed to the chapel door for three days.

"But daughter," he protested, blinking his watery eyes, "Church law proscribes a minimum of three weeks."

"I know, Father."

The kindly priest scratched his sparse gray hair. "A decent period of waiting is necessary, you know, so anyone with objections to the union will have time to come forward."

"I know," she said again.

All too well! There were any number of objections that could be brought. Consanguinity was often cited as grounds to bar or annul a marriage—even after fifteen years and two children, as with the King of France and his soon-to-be former wife, Eleanor. Rape, adultery, incest and murder by one party or another were also reasons to prevent or dissolve a marriage. Nor could any couple say their vows in time of fasting, such as Lent or Advent. Then there was the condition that caused her the most secret worry—that one or another of the parties involved might have taken monastic or religious vows.

Jocelyn still didn't know what had occurred at Blanche Garde. Odds were she would never know. She intended to take no chances, however.

"Three days, Father. Then I will take Sir Simon to husband either with your blessing or without."

The arrival of a royal courier that very evening forced her to scuttle those hasty plans. The message from King Baldwin informed Jocelyn that his cousin, Thomas of Beaumont, had lodged a complaint against her. His royal ward, it was alleged, had obstructed Sir Thomas in the performance of his duties as steward. The king himself would come to Fortemur to look into the matter. While there, he would stand witness to her marriage to Simon de Rhys. His mother, he added with magnificent understatement, had graciously deigned to accompany him. They would arrive ten days hence.

Within minutes of the courier's arrival, Lady Constance had thrown the entire keep into a frenzy of cleaning and cooking in preparation for the royal visit. Every bed curtain in the keep was carried outside and beaten to remove any hint of dust. Geese were mercilessly plucked for fresh feathers to fill bolsters.

Precious peppercorns and spices were brought from the storeroom to be ground with mortar and pestle. Hunters were sent to bag fresh game.

As the date approached, the ovens were raked out and fresh fires lit, while a small army of cook's assistants kneaded mounds of dough for bread and cakes. Suet puddings joined hams, and boars' heads in the cooking pots. The boards were scrubbed, and precious wax candles were placed in holders.

As chatelaine of the keep, Jocelyn kept every bit as busy as her people. Between consulting with Lady Constance on decisions ranging from what course to serve when, riding out with the hunters and harrying her ladies into completing the gown she would wear for the ceremony, she scarce had time to draw breath.

Simon stayed similarly occupied. Accompanied by Sir Guy, he inspected the armory, the gatehouses and guard posts. Before long, he knew the name of every pikeman who patrolled the curtain wall and every young, eager squire in training. He also recommended—and Jocelyn approved—a series of improvements to Fortemur's defenses. Included among those recommendations was one for the construction of stone watchtowers to replace the wooden pyres used to signal danger or potential attack. Ali ben Haydar's eldest son had not as yet launched any acts of reprisal for their father's death. They could yet come, however.

While all this was going on, Jocelyn's vassals began to arrive from near and far. As did the neighboring lords and ladies she'd invited to the festivities. The day before the king and his mother were to arrive, Fortemur was full to overflowing with guests from every corner of the kingdom.

So beset was Jocelyn from all sides that Lady Constance insisted she must needs slip away for an hour or two and breathe some sea air. She found the perfect opportunity to do just that when Sir Guy and Simon said they were going to inspect the first of the new watchtowers.

The tower sat atop the hill most directly above the keep. Others would stretch in an unbroken line the length of Jocelyn's domain, Sir Guy explained. Nodding, she gripped her skirts in one hand and used the other to steady herself while they climbed to the top. The men-at-arms who took turns standing watch day and night awaited them below.

The view from the circular platform at the top of the tower took her breath away. Gnarled and twisted olive trees stair-stepped up the rocky slopes behind. Before her, achingly blue Mediterranean stretched as far as the eye could see. And there, set atop a wall of bedrock washed by waves, Fortemur loomed solid and square.

This was the land that had bred her, Jocelyn thought fiercely as she breathed salty air into her lungs. This was where, pray God, she would breed strong sons and daughters. The perfume-drenched harem she'd been sentenced to but short weeks ago now seemed nothing but an evil dream.

Simon, too, breathed deep as his assessing gaze swept the shoreline. He, however, was more concerned with the tower's construction than with the unmatched beauty of the scene it provided. He thumped his foot on the planking, peered at the stones lining the fire pit and rapped a knuckle on the great iron cauldron that would send flames and smoke shooting into the sky day or night. With a grunt of approval, he turned to Fortemur's recently appointed castellan.

"The tower is well constructed, Sir Guy."

"As it should be," the older man acknowledged with a smile, "since it was done to your specifications."

Jocelyn could not but marvel at how easily her people had accepted Simon as their lord. Less than a fortnight ago, he'd sat below the boards with the lowest-ranking knights. Now he shared the high table with her, Sir Guy and Lady Constance. As far as she could tell, no one whispered or complained about his leap from minor knight to acknowledged lord of the keep.

Not that it would have made a difference if they had. Every day Simon showed another facet of his seasoned skill as a warrior. And every night...

Sweet heaven, the nights!

They'd delayed their wedding by royal command but not, thank the stars, their bedding. And if the nights to come held anywhere near the same incredibly erotic pleasure as the ones just past, Jocelyn might well expire of sheer, unadulterated pleasure. The mere thought of what the man could do with his clever, clever hands and mouth had her jerking on her reins.

As they approached the cliffs above Fortemur, she felt the need to have him to herself, away from the crowded keep, for a few moments more. What better place, she thought with a leap in her belly, than where he'd first taught her the joy a man could give a woman?

"I would speak with you," she told him. "Privately."

Her glance cut to the path that led down to the crystal cave, then came back again to his. The message she conveyed might have been emblazoned in gilt-edged script. Nor was it lost on Simon.

"Sir Guy," he said gruffly, "we'll see you back at the keep."

"Very well." The long-married knight guessed their intent and didn't bother to hide his smile. "But for God's sake, don't tarry too long or my lady wife will have my head."

Neither Jocelyn nor Simon paid him the least heed. She, because she'd already slipped from the saddle.

He, because his heart leaped straight into his throat when he saw her disappear below the cliff's edge.

Cursing, he tethered their mounts and negotiated the treacherous path. Each fragile step made his throat go drier. At every turn, he expected to see Jocelyn's broken body on the rocks below.

She was so headstrong, this woman he loved. So willful and determined. He would have his work cut out for him to tame her to his hand. But when he ducked through the cave's opening, all thought of changing or tempering her in any way fled.

As before, the salt crystals embedded in the walls reflected the sun in sparkling lights. For a moment or two, they blinded Simon to the vision that awaited him. Then his eyes adjusted to brilliance and he almost swallowed his tongue.

She'd already removed her gown, her undertunic, her stockings and shoes. Even her linen bellyband. Like a nymph just risen from the sea, she awaited him in unashamed, unadorned nakedness. His shaft was hard and aching before he so much as loosed his sword belt.

"Do you have any idea what you do to me?" he growled as he tugged his surcoat over his head.

"I've some small notion. But I most sincerely hope you will expound on the matter."

"Expound, be damned."

He tore at the ties to his mail shirt, thinking of how he'd drifted from pain to hope to pain again during the hellacious journey back to Fortemur. She was all he'd dreamed of during those torturous hours, all that had kept him in the saddle. He'd never envisioned her like this, though. His blood pounding as loud and as fast as the waves below, he couldn't rid himself of his garments fast enough.

Once naked, he swept her into his arms. Her mouth opened eagerly under his. Her breasts filled his hands with smooth, silken flesh. Their rigid tips ignited flames that burned hotter than any Greek fire when they pressed against him. Mouth to mouth, hip to hip, they fueled the passion that seared their souls.

"Do you know how you have filled my every waking moment?" He ground out the words, his mouth moving hungrily over hers. "My every thought?"

"No more than you've filled mine."

"I ache for you, Jocelyn."

He more than ached. He was damned near doubled over with wanting her. Every tendon and sinew in his body taut with need, he took her down atop their scattered clothing.

She opened for him eagerly. Lips. Arms. Thighs. With his blood roaring in his veins, he had to force himself to take the time to prepare her for his entry. Within moments she was panting. Moments more, and she was hot and wet and so slick he was able to thrust home with ease. Hooking her calves behind his, she canted her hips and took his full length with a clench of her belly muscles that popped beads of sweat out on Simon's brow.

Jocelyn welcomed him eagerly. Her head went back. Her breath rasped in her throat. His rigid length thrust in, out, in again.

He would not regret that he hadn't fulfilled his father's thrice-damned pledge, she vowed as pleasure gathered low in her belly. He would never regret it. She would not let him!

Then all thought fled. All ability to think fled. There was only his hard, slick body crushing hers. The hands buried in her hair to anchor her head as his mouth ravaged hers. The fierceness of his thrusts as he drove her higher, harder, faster.

"Simon!"

She tore her mouth from his, gasping as the tight swirls in her belly became dark, undulating waves. In the next breath, they built to a wild crest, then crashed and foamed and roiled, taking her with them. Her back arched. A groan ripped from far back in her throat. Every muscle in her body went taut with a pleasure so intense she near sobbed with it.

When the earth stopped swirling and righted itself again, she opened her eyes to find Simon staring down at her. He was still inside her. Still filling her. Muscles quivering, jaw working, he brushed the tangled hair from her face.

"That troubadour. Blondin. He didn't come near to capturing your beauty in his verses."

She managed a smile through her boneless lethargy. "Most like because he has not seen me as you have. With seaweed in my hair and my lips ablush from your kisses."

"Whatever happens," he said on a husky note, "whatever the years bring, I'll always remember you thus."

"Oh, so?" She willed her limp, satiated body back to life and wiggled provocatively. "It seems we're not done yet. Perhaps I'll provide you with other ways to remember me."

With a wicked glint in her eyes, she rolled atop him and splayed her hands on his chest. His tawny hair glinted with sweat. His blue eyes gleamed up at her.

She would remember this moment always, Jocelyn thought, silently echoing his words. Whatever came, whatever the years brought, this was the moment they joined forever. Slowly, so slowly, she raised her hips and brought them down again.

This time it was Simon who slumped limp and breathless to their scattered clothing. When his chest stopped heaving, he opened his eyes and almost glared at her.

"Will you ever surprise me like that, woman?"

"I'll do my very best. Now come." Imbued with

energy, she slapped his thigh. "We must needs return to the keep or Lady Constance will have our heads as well as Sir Guy's."

Chapter Sixteen

The queen who rode through Fortemur's gates alongside her son just before noon the next morning looked far different from the one Jocelyn had last spoken to. The Melisande she'd left at Blanche Garde had carried the ravages of a brutal battle on her face and in her voice. This one sat erect in her saddle. No worried grooves were etched into her face. No shadows darkened her eyes. A gem-studded coronet anchored her gossamer veil. Her gown was of the finest brocade and only lightly stained from travel. Its sleeves were so long their tasseled tips reached past her stirrups.

Jocelyn had dressed with no less care. Her maids had pinned her silvery-blond hair back in an intricate arrangement of braids and curls. She, too, wore a veil of the sheerest silk crowned with a circlet of beaten gold. Her gown was the one she'd had sewn for just this occasion. Cut square and low across her bosom, the moss-colored pile fell in graceful folds over an undertunic of golden, shimmering cloth.

Simon stood to her left. Jocelyn had set her ladies to sewing feverishly on his raiment as well as her own. They'd altered several of her grandsire's richest surcoats, but the one he wore this day she'd had cut and stitched especially for him. It was of red, trimmed at the neck and sleeve with the blackest ermine. Too hot for this sunny morning, mayhap, but he'd insisted on wearing Fortemur's colors when he took her to wife. The sight of him so tall and broad of shoulder, his sun-streaked hair freshly trimmed and his head held high, had her swelling with pride as they received their royal guests in the inner bailey.

Baldwin dismounted first and turned to assist his mother. While Melisande shook out her skirts, the king acknowledged Jocelyn with a gracious kiss on both cheeks.

"I didn't get to speak with you before you left Blanche Garde," he said to her, his expression serious. "My lady mother tells me you want this match as much as you did not want the last we'd arranged for you. Tell me now, before witnesses, if that's true."

"It's most definitely true, Majesty."

Nodding, he turned to Simon. "What about you, de Rhys? There's still time for you to change your mind. Are you sure you want to bind yourself to my ward?" A wry smile curved his lips. "If you haven't noticed it as yet, the Lady of Fortemur has a most stubborn will."

"I've noticed."

The drawled response drew a bark of laughter from the king. "And you still want her?"

"I do."

"Then I guess there's no hope for it, or for you."

Still chuckling, Baldwin offered his arm to his mother and gestured for Jocelyn to lead them inside. She'd prepared the lord's chamber for the king's use. The queen and her attendants she escorted to the ladies' bower. Lady Constance, bless her efficient soul, had ordered wine brought from casks in the deepest, darkest cellar. It was cool and light and perfect with the dish of olives, figs and cheeses she'd readied for their guests' refreshment.

While squires carried in the queen's traveling chests and her ladies busied themselves unpacking brushes and pots and gowns, Melisande sipped her wine and wandered to a recessed window embrasure. The shutters had been thrown back to let in the sea breezes. The wide ledge topped with the thick cushion that doubled as a sleeping mat provided a convenient resting spot.

Breathing in the clean, crisp air, she seated herself and patted the cushion beside her. "Come, girl, and sit with me. I would hear how you convinced de Rhys that he is more suited to marriage than to Holy Orders."

"I didn't, Majesty." Jocelyn sank down beside her on the thick cushion. "Simon was fully prepared to honor his vow. He completed every one of the initiation rituals," she related with a shudder she didn't try to repress.

"So I understand. The Grand Master could not speak to me of the matter, of course. God forbid I should tempt him to sin," Melisande said dryly. "Nor were any but the Templars present during the secret rites. But from what my son told me, de Rhys had to be carried from the chapel when they were done. And we think the Saracens barbarous," she added under her breath.

She shook her head before taking another sip of wine.

"If de Rhys completed the rituals, why is he here?"

"I don't know. He swore on his immortal soul never to reveal what occurred."

"And you, girl? Are you satisfied he didn't forswear himself? Do you believe in your heart of hearts that he still retains the honor you claim runs deeper in him than blood?"

Jocelyn's chin lifted. Absolute conviction rang in her reply. "I may doubt many things in this world, Majesty. I will never doubt Simon de Rhys."

A sigh feathered from the queen's lips. She let her glance stray to the sunlit waves outside the window embrasure. It lingered there for long moments before she brought her gaze back to Jocelyn.

"Would that I'd been given to a husband who would endure as much as de Rhys has for you. Count yourself beyond fortunate, lady. There are not many like him."

"Well do I know that, Majesty."

"Good. Now get you gone. I must rest a bit before I witness your exchange of vows."

When the king, too, had rested and refreshed himself, he instructed his chief scribe to produce the marriage contract he'd drawn up. The lengthy document detailed which rents and revenues would come to Simon and which Jocelyn would retain in her own name. As the king's ward, she would not ordinarily have been included in a review of this document. Baldwin possessed sole and legal right to dispose of her and her lands where he would. After Blanche Garde, however, the king suggested—and she heartily agreed—that she'd more than earned the right to know the disposition of both her person and her properties.

Then her vassals had to be gathered in the great hall to witness the signing of the contract. She'd invited every one of her knights and their ladies to Fortemur for the event that would affect their lives as much as hers. They would swear fealty to Simon in a separate ceremony following the marriage ritual.

For now, it was enough that they stood witness to this most essential transfer of rights and responsibilities, and that the three most senior among them signed or put their X below the king's signature.

They would witness, as well, the bedding to follow the wedding. Although Jocelyn didn't doubt that everyone from Sir Guy to the lowest stable boy knew Simon had shared her bed since his return to Fortemur, she wanted no question in anyone's mind that their union had been full and legally consummated.

Before going above stairs, she took time for a last, hurried conference with Lady Constance. Heads close together, they thrashed out the thorny questions of who to seat where at the boards and whether the parade of roasted swans should precede or follow the king's toast.

Finally it was time to ready for the exchange of vows! Breathless, she rushed up three flights of stairs to the ladies' bower. The queen awaited there, as did Jocelyn's ladies and maids.

Wielding comb and boar's-tooth brush, her maid attacked her braids and curls. Both she and the queen knew well she was no blushing virgin to so present herself, but appearances must be observed. When her gleaming, white-gold mane spilled down to the small of her back, one of Jocelyn's ladies pinched her cheeks to heighten their color. Another hastily stuffed wood chips soaked in costly musk into the gold pomander dangling from her girdle. Lady Constance rushed into the bower just in time to place a circlet of glossy green leaves interwoven with late-summer snow asters atop her veil.

"There," she decreed, swiping at an errant tear. "You're ready."

Queen Melisande looked the bride over from head to foot before nodding in assent. "She is indeed. Shall we descend to the chapel?"

With a rustle of skirts, the women made for the door. Before they reached it, a panting page burst through.

"Sir Simon sent me, lady. He asks if he might have private speech with you."

Jocelyn's stomach dropped. A tiny frisson of fear rippled along her veins.

"Now?" she asked.

"Yes, lady."

She flicked a quick, questioning glance at the queen. Melisande shrugged her assent.

"We'll await you below."

The page scurried off, the ladies filed out, and some moments later Simon appeared in the arched doorway.

"What is it?" Jocelyn asked, a tremor in her voice. "What's amiss?"

"Nothing's amiss," he hastened to assure her. "I came only to give you a bride gift."

She let out a shaky sigh. Her mental picture of

smoke rising from the new watchtower and a horde of heavily armed Saracens hurtling down the road toward Fortemur faded. Almost as quickly, another took its place.

This one was of a man chained and bruised and all but naked on the auction block. No one knew better than Jocelyn that he'd lost all on his journey to Outremer.

"Oh, Simon," she breathed. "I expect no bride gift."

"Nevertheless you shall have one."

He held out a hand and uncurled his palm. On it sat a glass pendant threaded on a black silk ribbon. It was in the shape of a chambered seashell, she saw with astonished delight, and crafted of the finest Venetian glass in the design known as *vitro-di-trina.*

The making of it was a closely guarded secret. Some said it resulted from fusing milk-white rods into clear glass. Others maintained the blower threaded tubes or canes into a bubble of molten glass. Whatever the method, the result was a delicate, lacy crystal that was prized by kings and queens throughout the world.

"Where did you find this?" Awed, she fingered the delicate shell. "And however did you get the funds to purchase it?"

"I saw it and others like it in a market stall in El-Arish, when we were being herded through the streets to the slave pens. It must have been booty taken from a captured Venetian galley. So when Queen Melisande gifted me with a hundred gold beasants for saving her life, I sent a troop of your men to El-Arish to purchase it for you. They returned but moments ago."

"Simon! Never say you paid a hundred beasants for a bit of glass!"

"Not quite. I have enough left to buy you a few gold and silver trinkets, as well." His mouth curved, then tipped in the wicked grin she'd come to know so well. "But every time you wear this particular trinket, I will think of our hours together in your crystal cave. So wear it often, wife."

Laughing, she bowed her head so he could tie the black ribbon around her throat. "Were it not for the hundred or more guests waiting for us below, I would thank you as you should be thanked."

The glint in his eyes deepened. "I'll remind you of that tonight, when the bed curtains rattle shut around us."

The shimmering pendant occasioned more than one envious glance when Jocelyn made her way to Fortemur's chapel. Father Joseph awaited them at the door, his seamed face wreathed in smiles. He'd yielded to her insistence that the banns didn't need to be posted for the full three weeks, but wouldn't be hurried in the reading of them now. His voice wavering and thin, he cited each condition that might prevent their marriage. After each, he paused for them to confirm the ban did not exist. Then he peered at the crowd gathered behind them, waiting to see if any objected to the union.

None did, but Jocelyn grew more nervous with each question. Surreptitiously, she fingered her crystal shell and dreaded the reading of the last of the banns.

"And are either of you bound by monastic or religious vows?" the priest asked, peering at them with his watery eyes.

"Not I," she answered swiftly.

Her fingers tightened on the delicate glass shell as she waited for Simon's response. He gave it in a clear, ringing voice.

"Nor I."

Jocelyn gulped and released the breath she only now realized she'd been holding.

"Then let us proceed to the vows."

Wetting his thumb, Father Joseph used it to fumble through his well-worn prayer book. His faded eyes squinted at first one page, then another, until the crowd shifted restlessly and an almost feverish impatience overtook Jocelyn.

Fate—or Satan in the form of Simon's dissolute father—had brought them together and come near to keeping them apart. She would be damned if she would allow fate or Satan in any form to play havoc with their lives now. As a result she said her vows in a feverish rush that made Father Joseph blink and Simon glance down at her with surprise.

Yes, she would take him to husband.

Yes, she would keep him and only him unto herself.

Yes, she would hold him for better or worse, for richer and for poorer, in sickness or in health, to be bonny and buxom at bed and board, to love and to cherish, till death them parted, according to God's holy ordinance.

And thereunto she plighted her troth!

"Er, well..."

Blinking owlishly, the castle priest turned to the groom. Simon said his vows in a more ordered fashion, and after he'd finished Jocelyn felt as though the weight of the world had been lifted from her chest.

It was done! Well and truly done! He was hers and she his. She could enter the chapel for the nuptial Mass with a light and joyous heart. Beaming as broadly as Father Joseph, she took her husband's arm.

The feasting that followed stretched for nigh on seven hours. The procession to the bridal bower that came later that night involved much laughter and hoots of encouragement. These lasted until Simon had removed his bride's jeweled garter, tossed it over his shoulder, and rattled the bed curtains shut amid ribald suggestions of how best to handle a wife as bold as his.

The celebration continued for several days. Jocelyn and Simon had arranged activities that included hunts, archery contests, jousts and boat races on sun-kissed seas. Before the guests departed, they showered the newly wedded couple with gifts. These ranged from a set of eighteen solid-gold goblets from Queen Melisande to a curved eating dagger from the lowest-ranking of Jocelyn's knights. She and her lord accepted all with equal gratitude.

Their most precious gift, however, did not arrive until almost six months later. It came in the form of a lean, dark-haired knight who appeared unannounced at Fortemur's gates with a squire and two spare horses.

Chapter Seventeen

Jocelyn didn't recognize the knight who was shown into the great hall that stormy winter's afternoon. She rose to greet him, but the pregnancy she'd announced so joyously just weeks before stirred an irritating swell of nausea in her belly. She had to stop and take several deep breaths to settle her rebellious stomach.

Simon caught her arm. His blue eyes raked her face. "Are you well, wife?"

"Well enough," she said with a rueful smile. "It's just your babe, making himself known. Go, greet our guest."

He strode the length of the hall with his long, sure stride and hooted with glee when the stranger threw back his rain-soaked hood.

"Robert de Burgh! You diseased son of a rag merchant."

It turned out Simon had once bested the man in the lists. Or he'd bested Simon, Jocelyn wasn't sure which, as they clasped hands and hammered each other's backs in the incomprehensible way of men.

"When did you arrive in the Holy Land?"

"Three days ago. I intended to go directly to Jerusalem, but when I heard that a certain Simon de Rhys had taken himself a lady to wife, I knew I must needs see for myself who would wed such a great lout as you."

Grinning, he turned to Jocelyn and made an extravagant bow.

"You'll understand my disbelief, lady, when I tell you of the many times this muscle-bound oaf and I stumbled back to our beds after a tourney or spent our last groat on—"

Simon growled a warning. "Robert."

"Very well. I won't disclose your many failings. Your lady has no doubt already discovered them herself."

Jocelyn couldn't help but laugh. "Indeed I have. I told Simon when first we met that he was not suited for the Church."

As soon as the words were out, she wished them back. She'd found joy and more happiness in these past months than she'd ever dreamed possible. The last thing she wished to do was remind her husband of the pledge that had caused them both such suffering and turmoil.

Other than a flicker of his eyes, Simon gave no sign that her words had struck home. His friend, however, looked utterly astonished.

"The Church? Never say you were thinking of becoming a monk!"

"I was, at one point."

"By all the saints," de Burgh exclaimed. "Why?"

Simon hesitated only briefly before replying. "My sire pledged me to the Knights Templar."

"Did he?" Still stupefied, de Burgh shook his head. "And to think Gervase said nothing of it when I asked about you. Only that you'd taken ship for the Holy Land."

"You spoke with him? Where? When?"

"Some two months ago, just before I departed. We competed against each other in a tourney hosted by the Count of Lille. Your sire took no prizes, by the way. He blamed it on the illness that had laid him low for some months before the tourney, but I think it due more to the fact that he spent his nights in Lille wenching and swilling ale with—"

He broke off, his eyes widening at Simon's fierce oath.

"Do you tell me my sire was wenching and swilling ale but two months ago?"

"Didn't I just say so?"

"By all the—!"

Simon spun on a heel and stalked away. Clearly

confounded, de Burgh looked from his rigid back to Jocelyn.

"I apologize most sincerely if I offended with my careless chatter. Let me assure you, Simon de Rhys is ten, nay, a hundred times the man his sire is."

"You didn't offend, sir. In fact, you have given us a gift more precious than you can know. Now I must attend to my lord."

She left the knight gaping at her in confusion and went in search of her husband. It took her some moments to find him. He was on the tower stairs that led to their chamber, staring through a window slit at the sea beyond. His shoulders were rigid and his jaw locked. Jocelyn said nothing as she came to stand beside him. She knew he must needs sift through his turbulent thoughts before he shared them with her.

If he shared them. She'd begun to wonder, when at last he blew out a breath and faced her. Outside the window slit, storm clouds shrouded the sea in shades of angry gray. Within the tower, the air carried a dank chill. Jocelyn didn't so much as feel its bite but Simon removed his fur-trimmed cloak and bundled it around her before he spoke.

"My father must have risen from his deathbed soon after I took ship for the Holy Land."

"So it would appear."

"Yet he sent no word."

"None that you know of," she agreed.

"Nor did he respond to the letter that my conscience

dictated I send, informing him that I had not joined the Templars."

"You know how long it takes for a missive to reach the West, if it gets there at all."

Although she spoke calmly, wrath burned in Jocelyn's breast. How like his thrice-damned father, she thought. To lay the burden of his sins on his son, then never bother to inform him that his most dire circumstances had changed. Gervase de Rhys had best hope he never came face-to-face with the woman his son had taken to wife!

But that was for some future day. Right now, the fact that the man had survived filled Jocelyn with nothing but relief.

"From the sound of it," she said cheerfully, "your sire's not yet done accumulating sins or penances."

Her light tone seemed to take her husband aback. Smiling at his startled expression, she laid her palms against his bristly cheeks.

"He will rot in hell or not. That's his choice. But you're free of him, Simon, now and forever more."

For the space of a heartbeat, mayhap two, she saw the merest hint in his eyes of all he'd endured because of his father's accursed pledge. Then the crooked grin she'd come to value as much as his strength of arm and heart put those dark memories away.

"You're right, wife. The only oath that binds me now is the one I made to you."

"And that, husband, you will never be free of."

She rose on her toes and brushed her mouth over his. Once, twice, as soft as a feather yet filled with a promise of more to come. They would have the life she'd dreamed of. They would have tall sons and laughing daughters. Here, in the land she'd been bred to and he'd come to love as much as she. That was all either of them could ask.

"Now," she told him, her voice and her heart brimming with love, "we'd best go back to the great hall. I would have this Robert de Burgh tell me more tales of the great lout I've taken to husband."

* * * * *

Author Note

While Jocelyn of Fortemur and Simon de Rhys are figments of my admittedly overactive imagination, many of the other characters in this book lived and breathed during the turbulent times of the Crusades.

Melisande reigned as Queen of Jerusalem from 1131 to 1152, when she relinquished authority to her son. She continued to serve as Baldwin's regent while he was on campaign until her death in 1161. The noted historian William of Tyre paid this remarkable queen the ultimate compliment of his times when he wrote that "she was a very wise woman, fully experienced in almost all affairs of state business, who completely triumphed over the handicap of her sex so she could take charge of important affairs…"

Her son, Baldwin III, proved a competent, if not brilliant, ruler. He recaptured several major cities and sought strategic alliances with powerful Christian supporters. To that end, he married Theodora, daughter of the Emperor of Byzantium. The marriage took place in 1158, when Baldwin was twenty-eight and Theodora thirteen years old. Baldwin died without heir in 1162, just a year after his mother's demise, and was succeeded by his younger brother, Almaric I.

Bernard de Tremelay was elected Grand Master of the Knights Templar in 1151. Two years later he and his knights participated in the siege of Ascalon. De Tremelay and about forty Templars were killed during the final battle and their heads sent to the sultan. When the Holy Land fell to the Saracens some years later, the Templars reestablished their order in Cyprus. However, their wealth and power had grown so great that they were resented both within the Church and without. In 1307, Philip IV of France—greatly in debt to the Templars—used charges of corruption and idolatry to arrest, torture and burn the warrior monks at the stake. He urged other Christian leaders to do the same, and in 1312 the Pope officially dissolved the order. Their mystique as some of the world's greatest warriors—and the persistent myth that they alone knew the whereabouts of the lost Ark of the Covenant—have persisted down through the ages.

COMING NEXT MONTH FROM

HARLEQUIN® HISTORICAL

Available July 26, 2011

- **THE GUNFIGHTER AND THE HEIRESS**
  by **Carol Finch**
  (Western)
- **PRACTICAL WIDOW TO PASSIONATE MISTRESS**
  by **Louise Allen**
  (Regency)
  (First in *The Transformation of the Shelley Sisters* trilogy)
- **THE GOVERNESS AND THE SHEIKH**
  by **Marguerite Kaye**
  (Regency)
  (Second in *Princes of the Desert* duet)
- **SEDUCED BY HER HIGHLAND WARRIOR**
  by **Michelle Willingham**
  (Medieval)
  (Second in *The MacKinloch Clan* family saga)

Once bitten, twice shy. That's Gabby Wade's motto—
especially when it comes to Adamson men.
And the moment she meets Jon Adamson her theory
is confirmed. But with each encounter a little something
sparks between them, making her wonder if she's been
too hasty to dismiss this one!

Enjoy this sneak peek from ONE GOOD REASON
by Sarah Mayberry, available August 2011
from Harlequin® Superromance®.

Gabby Wade's heartbeat thumped in her ears as she marched to her office. She wanted to pretend it was because of her brisk pace returning from the file room, but she wasn't that good a liar.

Her heart was beating like a tom-tom because Jon Adamson had touched her. In a very male, very possessive way. She could still feel the heat of his big hand burning through the seat of her khakis as he'd steadied her on the ladder.

It had taken every ounce of self-control to tell him to unhand her. What she'd really wanted was to grab him by his shirt and, well, explore all those urges his touch had instantly brought to life.

While she might not like him, she was wise enough to understand that it wasn't always about liking the other person. Sometimes it was about pure animal attraction.

Refusing to think about it, she turned to work. When she'd typed in the wrong figures three times, Gabby admitted she was too tired and too distracted. Time to call it a day.

As she was leaving, she spied Jon at his workbench in the shop. His head was propped on his hand as he studied blueprints. It wasn't until she got closer that she saw his

HSREXP0811

eyes were shut.

He looked oddly boyish. There was something innocent and unguarded in his expression. She felt a weakening in her resistance to him.

"Jon." She put her hand on his shoulder, intending to shake him awake. Instead, it rested there like a caress.

His eyes snapped open.

"You were asleep."

"No, I was, uh, visualizing something on this design." He gestured to the blueprint in front of him then rubbed his eyes.

That gesture dealt a bigger blow to her resistance. She realized it wasn't only animal attraction pulling them together. She took a step backward as if to get away from the knowledge.

She cleared her throat. "I'm heading off now."

He gave her a smile, and she could see his exhaustion.

"Yeah, I should, too." He stood and stretched. The hem of his T-shirt rose as he arched his back and she caught a flash of hard male belly. She looked away, but it was too late. Her mind had committed the image to permanent memory.

And suddenly she knew, for good or bad, she'd never look at Jon the same way again.

Find out what happens next in ONE GOOD REASON, available August 2011 from Harlequin® Superromance®!

HSREXP0811